The Legend of V

Book 1
The Solar System's Prophecies

by Varak Kaloustian

First published by Dog Ear Publishing
4011 Vincennes Rd
Indianapolis, IN 46268
www.dogearpublishing.net

ISBN: 978-0-9987-7732-0

This book is printed on acid-free paper.

This book is a work of fiction. Places, events, and situations in this book are purely fictional and any resemblance to actual persons, living or dead, is coincidental.

Printed in the United States of America

CONTENTS

CHAPTER 1

The Ultimate Tragedy

It was unbelievable. The pain, the grief, the sorrow, and the loss. Even though it was six years ago, I remember the moment like it was yesterday. In an instant, my life was changed. It was a cold, winter day. I was only seven and on winter break, enjoying a well-deserved respite from the second grade - playing with my favorite little red doll. My mom and dad were making dinner for the five of us: me, my mom and dad, and my brothers, Z and D. My name is V. I've got a medium sized Afro, brown eyes, and I'm about five-ten now, but was a good foot shorter back then. I'm the middle of the three brothers, with Z being the oldest, and D the youngest.

After about an hour, dinner was ready, and all of us were at the table. If I had known my life was about to be taken away at that instant, I would've kissed my family goodbye. But, even in retrospect, I'm glad I didn't know. In five seconds, my life was about to change. Five...four... three...two...one...BOOM! A huge explosion tore through my house and rocked the entire neighborhood.

After the blast, my family wasn't with me anymore. I panicked. Crying, I searched the entire house but didn't find them until I reached the decimated front door. My entire family was concealed inside of a floating, distorted purple ball. I was about to ask if they were okay, but was silenced by fear when another person that wasn't a part of my family walked toward me. To send more jitters down my spine, this sixth person looked exactly like me, except with red eyes, dark blue hair with an up-side-down "V" like figure going through it, and an evil smirk on his face.

I sensed a dangerous vibe off of him immediately.

"Wh-who...are you?"

His reply... I still haven't forgotten a single word after six years. The figure said, "V, you're next. And then it's your entire galaxy. I'll be back for you." He vanished, dragging the purple ball with him. My family - Mom, Dad, Z, and D were all gone, kidnapped. Terrified, I had no idea what to think. I felt so helpless and useless, like my life was on strings. Knowing some stranger was out there, and would be back for me. I wished I could vanish from the face of the Earth right then instead of delay my inevitable demise. I was so lost. As if in a trance, I went looking for my best friend who lived next door. It turns out, he was the only other one I knew who survived the blast. Griff, also seven, is an only child, so he's quite independent. He is very trustworthy, caring, and adventurous. He has brown eyes, and long, straight hair. His parents had gone missing too.

"I'm scared Griff!" I reached out to hug him.

"Me too!"

We cried sooty tears until the police arrived. After they patiently calmed us down, we finally explained what happened. They initially thought we were making things up, but when they saw that our parents were actually missing, they started paying closer attention. I don't blame the police for not believing us at first. Frankly, would you believe that someone who looked exactly like me train-wrecked the entire neighborhood and then took our families? I didn't think so.

When my eyes cleared, I saw that one of the policemen wore a warm and welcoming smile on his face. His name is Rodger. He was so nice to us, and very caring. He is still an enigma to me. Without asking a single question, he became our legal guardian so we wouldn't have to go to an orphanage.

Reconstruction on the neighborhood began soon thereafter. I asked the police if they could build a tree house for Griff and me. They agreed because they wanted to help alleviate our pain in any way possible.

After the tragedy, things went downhill even more. I changed from my happy-go-lucky self to a more depressed, reserved type person.

The four-year time period after my parents disappeared was the worst time of my life.

On an average day, I would wake up, get a pep talk from Rodger about not feeling down about my parents and that something would eventually turn up, commute half an hour to school, get teased and harassed, and go home knowing that the exact same thing was going to happen again the next day. No one understood, ever, but Rodger at least tried to help. Sadly, Griff shared my same fate. We spent the days together in a corner, around the only fire we had. Our care for each other kept us warm and comfortable.

So how did I get to where I am today? It started one day in sixth grade. I had a chance to put the class bully in his place. I'd had enough of the teasing after several years, so I decided to take matters into my own hands. The bully was hanging out in the same corner as Griff and me. His little gang and he were whispering and giggling about something. During their conversation, I heard Griff's and my name mentioned. I went up to the bully, who was much bigger than me, and somehow found the strength to knock him down.

"That should teach you!"

"Do you honestly think anyone cares about you?"

He rolled to his feet and threw a punch, which started a fistfight.

Griff hurried over and tried to stop the fighting, but while he was a little stronger than me, he was no match for the monstrous monolith that was staring us down. The bully knocked Griff to the ground, and at that point, I'd had enough. I thought one way I could possibly defeat him was to get a crowd behind me. I limped to the center of the quad area where everyone could see. They gasped at the sight of me.

"What's the matter?" One girl yelled. "Did you get caught in a garbage disposal?"

"Actually," I glanced toward her as the bully slowly approached. "Th-that's not too far off."

"WHY YOU LITTLE...!" The bully circled behind and kicked me hard in the back. My back hurt, but not as much as my face and arms, which were black, blue, and red. I couldn't take another blow.

At that moment a supervisor finally spotted me. "That's quite enough!" She picked me up. "Oh dear, he needs help."

"He only needs help when I say he does!" The bully walked up to the supervisor and kicked me out of her arms.

"Maybe this'll finally teach V that his sorry attitude isn't welcome here," a boy yelled from the side.

Just then, someone came up from behind him, and smashed the bully in the head. He hit him so hard, that the bully immediately fell to the ground, unconscious. As he fell, I saw a blurry image of my best and only friend.

Griff said, "No, V just doesn't welcome YOUR sorry butts. That's why he has no friends here, except me."

"That's not saying much, considering you're like brothers," another girl yelled out of the crowd.

"SO?" Griff yelled in an authoritative voice - as authoritative as an eleven year old can get - "I'm also the only one who ever gave V a chance at friendship. You jerks are so self-centered. You don't care about anyone else but yourselves! Look at this guy. He's been through so much, but instead of showing compassion and letting him just be a kid and have fun, you act like he's the one that disappeared. Does he look like he'd ever do you any harm?"

"Disappear? What are you talking about?" Nelly yelled.

Someone came up behind Griff. "We don't need friends like you!"

Griff got shoved on top of me.

"That's enough, you bullies!" A voice from a megaphone came from a distance. As the figure got closer, I was relieved to see it was Rodger.

That's when I lost consciousness.

"W-what?" The bully backed up. "What's this police officer doing here?"

"Only picking up my kids." Rodger whipped out his Tonfa. Everyone gasped, backing up.

"HA! You can't hurt me. It's against the law."

"But you'll walk away knowing that you senselessly assaulted a minor who just wanted some friends. Is that really too much to ask? Look at this boy." Rodger's eyes started to water. He picked me up and held me high in the air. "Does this kid look like such a bad guy to you? Just give him a chance! Have any of you really talked to him?"

Some chatter arose.

Rodger continued. "I know he's been feeling despair from the kidnapping of his family and the fact that some life form can possibly be hunting him down, but I had no idea that he was being harassed here too. It seems he's gotten really good at hiding his feelings. He's so scared that he doesn't even want to talk to the people that care about him most. Go home now, all of you! IN THE NAME OF THE LAW, THIS SCHOOL IS CLOSED TODAY!"

Whispers arose about what Rodger had said about my family and the mystery figure.

"Really?" one boy said. "No wonder..."

"Poor thing. Just look at him." Another pointed from a distance.

"You can't close down a place of education." One of the teachers started toward Rodger.

Rodger swiftly turned his head toward the teacher. "For being a danger to public safety, I can. Look at my child! This school needs some serious rehabilitation. Until this dungeon provides a safe environment, it is closed."

With that, Griff carried me and we left school.

"Just hang in there V, I'll get you to a hospital right away," Rodger said. "You're not going to set foot in that deathtrap again. Griff, did you know about..."

Rodger just dropped the question and focused on rushing us to the nearest emergency room.

Griff was crying so much my shirt became a damp sponge. "V, please just survive. You're the only family I have left." Griff poured his heart out. And yes, he said survive. I was in terrible condition. It turned out I had three broken ribs, and a fractured leg. I felt like I was about to die physically, but I could feel my mind and spirit rising with strength for the first time in years. I realized I don't want to vanish. I want to make my life meaningful. I want to cleanse the world of anything like that bully and his iron fist.

Luckily, the doctors took great care of me, and Rodger was by my side the entire time. I stayed in the hospital for several days because I could barely move. I was sent home in a giant body cast and an air bed. The tree house didn't have an elevator. Luckily, the ambulance I was transported in had a conveyor belt on the top, so I was taken from the back of the truck, carried to the top, and rolled into the tree house. I remained in the exact same spot for about two weeks until I could at least be moved around in a wheelchair.

After I completely recovered, I was assigned to a new school. I was nervous to be going back because I realized that since my family vanished there had never been any kid who really understood me except for Griff. He cared so much for me that he was willing to throw himself in front of the bully to protect me. It seemed like kids don't really want to spend time getting to know someone if they are really sad. Maybe that's why some kids who are sad turn aggressive and end up bullying nicer kids themselves. Sitting with only Griff again at lunchtime I thought to myself, "Here we go, again".

However, this time was different.

Her name was Azilez. I'll never forget her kindness. Her smile was the first thing I noticed. She radiated happiness just by being there. It was a comforting feeling knowing that someone outside of my own family had come up to me and wholeheartedly smiled.

"Are you okay?" Azilez asked in a calm tone. Right then and there, I became aware that it's possible to have someone show concern toward me. That was the first time someone, a stranger, had given me a chance to be her friend.

"Why do you care?" were the words that came out of my mouth.

She took a step back and held her heart in astonishment. "What's wrong?"

"I said why do you care?" I retorted in a frustrated and confused tone. I can't explain all the emotions I was feeling in that moment. I recall feeling a bit overwhelmed and I honestly wanted to know why she cared. No one had ever shown concern for me, except for my family, and I thought they only did that to make me feel better.

Now she got a little mad.

"What's your problem?"

I fell on the blacktop and started to cry. At the sight of this, Azilez realized there was something really wrong and ran to get help from her friends. Within minutes, about ten other people came and surrounded me. My face had streaks of black running across it. My tears were erasing the composite material.

"What's that kid's problem?" one of the boys asked.

"I asked the same thing," Azilez said. "But when I did, he just started bawling. I think something's seriously wrong. Kids just don't normally act like this in public."

"I guess you're right. Should we get him to talk?"

"No I don't think that'll work. Now that I think about it..." Azilez scratched her chin. "Hmm.... I think I've got it. Everyone, come here!"

All the kids huddled and started whispering amongst themselves. When I saw them in a circle formation, I thought they were just making fun of me. After they finished, they dispersed throughout the campus and went to their next classes. I got up and proceeded to do the same.

After all of my classes finished, I got picked up by Rodger and headed home. When I climbed up the tree house and opened the door, I was shocked to see the same eleven people that I had seen at school earlier that day.

"What do you want? Actually, first, who are you? I never got your name."

The girl walked out of the crowd of people and introduced herself: "My name is Azilez. I never really picked up your name, either. Well, what is it?"

"Wow, you're quite persistent. V. My name is V."

"That's a cool name." She giggled a little bit.

"You're really starting to confuse me. Why do you care about me so much? It's not like I matter to you."

"Actually, you seemed pretty miserable back at school, so we just came to hang out and get to know you better."

I shook my head to make sure I was hearing her correctly. "But no one cares about me except my own family. And that doesn't mean much anymore."

Azilez's hand went to her mouth. Her eyes widened in compassion and amazement. "What? Who told you that?"

I tried to hold back tears. "Well, everyone I've ever met, except my family. But they're not even my real family..."

"What happened to your real family?"

The moment Azilez asked, my loss seemed too much to handle and I broke down again.

"Okay. You don't have to tell me." She ran over, picked me up, and then did something I will never ever forget. Azilez gave me a hug. I slowly put my arms around her too. It was the first true moment of happiness I'd had since I lost my family to that mystery man. I felt so alive.

After I got a grip, I wiped my eyes and actually cracked a smile. "Thank you, Azilez."

I noticed that Griff, looking amazed, was standing at the front door. "Uh, who are these people?" he asked.

Up to that point, Griff really hadn't had a friend besides me, so having other people at the tree house was a bit of a shock to him.

I grabbed his shoulder and felt relieved to say: "Friends, Griff. They're our friends."

Griff suddenly smiled at the thought of having friends again.

I then glanced toward Azilez. "I'll tell you everything. It's story time." Trusting and feeling comfortable around my new friends, I felt myself regain the personality I had lost along with my family. We sat down and Griff and I told our newfound friends everything that had happened to us up to that point, including the mystery man.

"Are you serious?" One of the other girls seemed skeptical.

"I know it's really hard to take in, but imagine living with this the last four years of your life. Can you imagine the impact it would have on you? All Griff and I really needed were friends. We never had any until now. Thanks guys."

And with that, the present-day V and Griff are born. We still keep in touch with the entire group. But to this day, Azilez has been my best friend, along with Griff.

In the present, Griff and I are thirteen years old, and Rodger is STILL our legal guardian. Rodger is pretty short for his age, but he's strong. He has blue eyes the color of the ocean, and medium length, black hair. He has a short body, but a big heart and spirit. Rodger tells us that the mystery person hasn't appeared at all after our neighborhood was destroyed, which is bad news since he's our only connection to our families. However, he does tell us that the search party that was sent for all the parents and children that went missing did find something only recently. They found that Egypt's famous creation, the Great Sphinx, is acting like it's alive. That is just downright creepy.

"Is that confirmed, Rodger? Is it even possible?" I ask.

"It's not confirmed, but some people have said they've seen it move. No one wants to believe them, but the number of witnesses is increasing by the day. As impossible as it seems, I think there's a solid possibility that it is alive. In fact, I was planning to go check it out myself."

I wonder if the Sphinx can actually come to life. And if it is possible, how did it come to life?

Later that day, in the tree house, I share my thoughts with Griff to see if it's actually worth leaving home and going to check this out.

"Should we go to Egypt, Griff?"

"If there's a possibility that we can find our parents, along with everyone else that was abducted that day, then absolutely, I'm game."

"All right then." I smile. "Let's tell Rodger that we want to go."

Griff thinks for a few seconds then stops me from heading to the phone. "Wait, V! What about Azilez?"

"No! I don't want to put her in harm's way. This is between Rodger, us, our families, and the figure that took them." I decide to wait until Rodger gets home to tell him Griff's and my decision in person. When he returns from work, we tell him that we should all go together to see the Sphinx in person. He likes the idea and the three of us prepare to go.

Griff and I take a backpack and about 500 yards of rope, duct tape, and other handy supplies that Rodger brought from work. Rodger takes his sweet utility belt that's got really cool things in it, like his Taser and Tonfa. It's finally time for our new adventure to begin.

CHAPTER 2

The Mystery Person's Hideout

Griff, Rodger, and I make it to Egypt. Weird events have already begun to occur because when we get there, nobody is at the airport.

"Now that's creepy," Rodger begins, "when I came here months ago with the squad to check if your parents are here, this area was teeming with people."

"Well this could probably mean that the rumor we heard about the Sphinx, I am shocked to say, is probably not a rumor at all...."

"That's not good!" Griff sure has a way of simplifying things.

"No," Rodger says, "not at all, Griff."

"Let's go to the Sphinx. Now!"

Griff and Rodger agree. We rush to the Sphinx. As we make our way through the city of Cairo, I search for signs of human life, but I don't find a single soul.

"Hey guys," I call as we're still running. "Have you noticed that there's no one in this ENTIRE city?"

Griff and Rodger take a moment to stop and scan their surroundings. The more the two observe, the more their eyes widen.

"Impossible!" Griff stands stunned. "How can a heavily populated city like Cairo just not have any people anymore? I highly doubt this is the Sphinx's doing."

"Then it must be..." I close my eyes to think it over.

"The mystery man," Rodger conjectures as he completes my thought. "It has to be."

"Then the faster we get there, the better," Griff starts to run as fast as he can. "Come on!"

The Great Sphinx of Giza was built thousands of years ago with a lion's body and man's face. It is the largest structure ever created from a single piece of stone. Its paws alone are 50 feet long. It's been damaged over the years and has a missing nose, or so I've read in books. When we get to Giza, we are shocked to see the monumental structure has a full-grown nose and glowing, green eyes. It is alive!

"Oh God!" Griff murmurs. "How are we supposed to take down an oversized cat?"

"You tell me," Rodger says. "Like I'm going to know. That thing is taller than a six-story building! Actually, give me a sec...."

"NO!" the Sphinx roars.

"It talks?" Griff is flabbergasted.

I'm just as stunned as Griff, but at the same time, exhilarated. I mean, how can I not be? I'm literally talking to a piece of ancient history! But at the same time, it does look quite intimidating. I have to be quick on my feet. There's no telling when this thing will just swat us with its giant paw.

"Yes," the Sphinx says, "I have been reborn by a mystery figure that looks like you, V!"

I'm guessing that the Sphinx caught my name because of the mystery guy, but I'm still wondering how the mystery person himself knows my name.

"Wait, you mean..."

"Yes, the so-called 'figure' you know is my creator!"

"Wait," Griff cuts in, "what about my parents?"

"I don't know what you're talking about, but that's beside the point. You won't get past me. I know what you want to do with this legacy of yours, and I'm not letting it happen!"

"Wait," I cautiously walk toward it. "What are you talking about?"

"RRRRROOOOOAAAARRRR!" The Sphinx stirs up a sandstorm with a malevolent roar. The grit of the sand rakes across our skin and the dust makes it hard to breathe.

I guess this means that we're going to have to take down the Sphinx before we get to the mystery man. It might know something about his location. We're going to have to make it talk, so we can't destroy it.

It's a long shot, but I have an idea. "Griff, Rodger, I've got a plan. Rodger, what if we use your whip to tame the beast?"

"That'll never work," Griff says over the sandstorm. "The whip's not long enough!"

"I know. But what if we use the long rope we brought and attach the whip at the end of it?"

"I'm not sure it'll work," Rodger shouts. "But it's all we've got. Let's do it!"

As we're about to attack, the Sphinx pounces first. It tears the rope in half, which sends us flying. The Sphinx is ready to finish us off. But as it's charging, it stops, and takes a good, long look at me. Then, it does an astonishing thing. Its eyes widen, it stops the storm and kneels before me. What's going on?

"That thing is evil. It tricked me! My apologies, V and friends, you may pass."

We have so many questions, but at that moment we are all so relieved the Sphinx doesn't want to crush us or eat us alive. So we don't ask. We just run past the beast.

"That was...odd," I state the obvious still in shock.

"What?" Griff looks over. "The fact that the Sphinx is alive, or that it just knelt before us?"

"Yeah, both really. But that second one. What could it have remembered that caused it to do that?"

"I don't know. I'm just glad to be alive!"

After a while, we reach the Great Pyramid of Giza. There is a bright light coming out of it.

"Explanation, anyone?"

"Your guess is as good as mine, V," Rodger says. "I have no idea how or why that's happening."

"Griff? Anything?"

"I'm in the same boat as Rodger."

"Great." Suddenly, I feel an incredible force crashing down on me like a tidal wave.

    –V...

    –What the...? Who, or for that matter, what, are You?

    –I'll be waiting on the other side of that light. I have the answers you seek...

    –Seek about what? What is this? How is this happening? How are You in my thoughts?

    –You're saying that like you have NO IDEA about your legacy...

    –That's because I don't! What answers do You have? And how do I know this isn't a trick by the mystery man?

    –Because I can see where he is from up here...

    –What? What does that mean?

But It vanished. The life around me feels dead like it did when I first stepped into Cairo. "Let's go, guys."

"To that light? I don't know if that's a good idea." Rodger, our guardian, says.

"I'm all in. If it's fine by V, then it's fine by me!"

"Oh dear..." Rodger regretfully follows us.

As we get close enough, we start to feel a strong electromagnetic force around us. The force is so powerful that it makes us vanish into thin air. Are we dead? I pinch myself. I'm still able to move, feel, and think so definitely not, but it does feel like I'm dreaming because what we see next, I'm pretty sure no human has ever seen before. There is a strange star pattern. I see what looks like a moon, but it's quite dim and bloated. It's much darker than usual. I'm not sure what that force was. It wasn't strong enough to be a black hole, but whatever it was, it was able to transport us billions of miles away to a dark castle.

"Whoa..." I'm overwhelmed and amazed. I recognize this place. We're next to Pluto! I have always had an interest in space because I love its everlasting mystery. There's always something new to explore. But when you see space in person, that's an experience like nothing else.

Wow! It's breathtaking. Oh no...AIR! Wait, I can breathe. Somehow Griff and Rodger are not gasping for air or freezing to death either.

"What's going on?" I look at Griff and Rodger. "How are we not freezing to death or suffocating?"

"I have no idea." Rodger says, confused and in shock.

"Where are we and how'd we get here?" Griff asks as he walks off to start exploring.

"We must be on an asteroid next to Pluto. That huge object in the sky is Charon, Pluto's moon. It looks dim because it's reflecting sunlight and the sun is really far away right now. It should be freezing cold though. And I have no idea how we got here so fast."

"Does it really matter? I have a better question... How do we get back home?" Rodger yells hysterically.

"But I want to know how we're even breathing out here. It could be a major breakthrough!" I continue to think out loud.

We are so preoccupied with actually being here, Rodger and I miss the obvious.

"Uh, V." Griff tugs my shirt. "Look over there." I would recognize him anywhere. He looks exactly the same, even after six years. It's the mystery figure!

"Glad to see you, V," the figure says. "But it doesn't look like you're very happy to see me. HAHAHAHAHA!"

"You fiend! What have you done to Griff's and my families?"

"Oh, them. They were a real bother."

"What have you done to them?"

"I tossed them aside...to oblivion! BWAHAHAHAHAHA! You won't see them for a while. Actually, you will, V. You're going there too!"

I feel no fear. Rage and resentment, but not fear. "Not on my watch! Let's do this, whatever-your-name is!"

"My name is Vizor, and I'm here to wipe you off the face of this universe!"

"All right, Vizor, I've been itching to get to you for years."

"Looks like you have a death wish. Very well, I'll be happy to grant it! Let the battle begin."

Vizor wastes zero time trying to kill us. He rushes toward Griff, Rodger and me using the upside-down "V" like figure in his hair as a sword. Wow, I didn't know he could do that. Still, since there are three of us we spread out and start to overwhelm him. Getting desperate, Vizor uses a mind control technique to take control of my friends' minds. The enemy possesses them and they actually turn against me! I know it's not really them but it still feels awful to have the people I trust and love look like they want to annihilate me. But while they are in that condition, I notice something glowing in the background. It looks like a floating, radiating tablet. Is that the light that will get us back to Earth? Then another possibility comes to mind. What if it's the source of Vizor's mind control power? There's only one way to find out. It's a long shot, but I use all the strength I have to jump and grab it.

"Oh no you don't!" Vizor whips out a grappling hook from his hair and grabs my foot with it. How many tricks does this guy have in his hair? As I hit the ground, Vizor moves toward me. "That's right...sit there like the little helpless puppy you are." He's still holding the hook. This gives me an idea.

"Gotta run, Vizor!"

"Hey! Where do you think you're going?"

Yes! The grappling cord is stretched out. Now's my chance!

"RUF, RUF!" I jump and the stretched cord helps me fly toward Vizor at an incredible velocity. Upon impact, I make him release his grip, and send him flying.

While Vizor is down, I grab the shining object. A radiant surge fills my friends and the castle. My friends are freed of Vizor's grasp. They pin him down.

"We want answers," I bludgeon.

"Ugh..." Vizor says. "For what?"

"This tablet," I point out the obvious. "What is it?"

"That tablet is one of the five legendary Solar Prophecies..."

"Solar Prophecies? What's it supposed to do?"

"Are you sure you want to know?" he asks.

I raise an eyebrow and Vizor knows we mean business. "That's not all I want to know..."

"Okay. Having possession of one will give someone a certain

power. Having two, three, or four, will give them even more power, depending on which prophecy they have. If one obtains all five, they will acquire great power, especially if..."

"If what?" Rodger says tightening his grip on Vizor. "Speak up!"

"Especially if you are the chosen one."

"But why were you trying to hide this prophecy from us?" I finally realize what all of this has to do with...

"Because, V... You are the chosen one!"

CHAPTER 3

The Five Solar Prophecies and Vizor's Horrid Plan

Say that again, Vizor. I'm the chosen one? When was this established? Griff and Rodger still have Vizor pinned down because we want to know more. Like why he took Griff's and my family. We want to know where they are so that we can rescue them from Vizor's evil clutches. Also, we need to know how and where we can get our hands on the rest of these prophecies because they seem important, especially if I'm "the chosen one". If they do give me power, then we're going to need them to defeat Vizor and his master plan. But all the while, there's a burning question running through my mind: Why am I some "chosen one"?

"All right, Vizor. You have a lot to say, but we don't have a lot of time. Spill out everything you know, NOW!" He hesitates, but Griff and Rodger hold him even tighter.

"ARRGGHH!" Vizor screams in pain. "Fine. I took both of your parents for a reason. V, I wanted your parents more because they have known about your ancient legacy. I took everyone else in the surrounding area to cover my tracks."

I cut him off there. "Did you take their lives?"

"Why would I do that when I could kidnap them instead? Why set their souls free when I can keep them in eternal torment? HAHA-HAHA!"

"WHAT HAVE YOU DONE TO THEM?" Rodger gives him a nice squeeze.

"Where are they?" I scream, holding back with all of my will.

"For your sake, Vizor, I hope my parents are safe!" Griff starts to squeeze a bit harder.

"Arghhh!" Vizor screams in pain. "You guys don't have such a bad grip. I can't say they're safe, but I can guarantee they're alive."

–Ugh! Keep your cool, V. You still have more questions to ask... "What is my legacy? And why am I some 'chosen one'?"

"You're telling me your parents never mentioned that important little fact? Ha! That's a laugh."

"Tell us what this legacy of V's is," Rodger demands, "or I'll have my fists do it for you!"

"Okay, okay. This legacy goes back to the creation of the world. I don't know much about it, but I do know where you can find out more. It is hidden on Pluto somewhere. But I'm not sure where..."

–Don't get sucked into his lies, V. A voice pops in my head.

–What was that? Who is this?

–It's me, the prophecy!

–You can talk and think normal thoughts?

–Yes. I know it's abnormal for a tablet to do so. Don't worry. I'm just happy I'm not being used to control innocent people's minds!

–That's awesome! Nice to meet you. And thanks for the info.

–Anytime, V.

"I don't buy it, Vizor."

"Buy what?"

"How do you know the answers I seek are on Pluto, but you don't know WHERE on Pluto? There's hardly anything there to begin with."

"I guess you'll figure it out eventually. The answers you seek lie in the Cave of Destiny on the very top of Pluto."

This is all so fascinating.... To think there's this legacy revolving around me. Why have I not known about this?

"Cave of Destiny?" Rodger is surprised. "I never knew Pluto held such deep secrets."

I take a closer look at Pluto, and see that there's no sign of a cave. Maybe it's hidden? I still have a feeling Vizor's not telling us everything.

"Why are you so hesitant, Vizor?"

"What do you mean?"

"You're still not telling us everything. You said there's this cave on Pluto, but there clearly isn't anything there."

"Do you honestly expect me to know EXACTLY where it is?"

"Well you seem to know SO MUCH about it. So yes, we do."

"Heh. You're good at this little game. It doesn't appear to just anyone, you know. The Cave of Destiny is a very well kept secret."

"Then to whom does it appear?"

"A chosen few that it thinks are important."

"How does a cave know who's who?" Griff questions.

"That, I truly don't know."

–V, he's lying again.

–Thanks for that. I was just about to ask you if he was or not.

"You're a terrible liar, you know that Vizor?"

"You clearly know there's something in there that senses the presence of others." Griff adds.

"I swear it's the cave itself. It holds the very spirits of V's ancestors. That's all I know!"

"Who are these ancestors of mine and why are they so important?"

"I don't know that. The cave does. The spirits of your ancestors are there."

–Okay this time he really doesn't know.

"Fine, fine. I'll bite. One last question: Why did you have that prophecy when it's obviously connected to me?"

"I have the Prophecy of Wisdom because I am trying to collect all of the Solar Prophecies to destroy the Milky Way Galaxy with the negative energy that I possess. Then, I will rebuild the galaxy with the positive energy of the Solar Prophecies. I will avenge my home planet!"

"You lost us again," Rodger replies. "Home planet? Avenge? Did something happen?"

Vizor shudders like an animal that's lost in a rainstorm when we ask him to explain what happened to his home planet, but he answers.

"Years ago, my own galaxy and solar system were in peace and harmony. But then, that all changed. A portal to Hell appeared and took the entire galaxy, and my family - my mom, dad, and brother, X - were all taken by the Devil. I can bring them back but, of course, that means I'll have to eliminate this galaxy. Oh well. I guess that's life, V."

"You call that life? Why do you HAVE to destroy THIS galaxy?"

"Because your galaxy and mine are linked. My galaxy is literally the shadow of your galaxy. Only the Milky Way has the energy I need to tear into Hell and get my galaxy back!"

So Vizor's an alien from a galaxy that is supposedly the shadow of mine? That explains how he has a grappling hook and a sword-like "V" in his hair. But then Rodger and Griff squeeze Vizor so hard he literally melts. Which is shocking enough, but then he spontaneously reappears as if nothing happened! That's enough to show us he's an alien.

"Oh the benefits of being an Omoh Sapien. I'll see you guys around."

"Omoh Sapien? What is that? The opposite of a human?" But he just vanished. I guess that means we won this battle? Still, I have a feeling that it was going to be one of many.

CHAPTER 4

Vizor's Castle

take a moment to recap everything that just happened. Apparently, I'm the chosen one and I'm supposed to gather these Solar Prophecies and use them before Vizor tries to destroy and rebuild the Milky Way Galaxy.

He wants to avenge the loss of his home planet that the Devil maliciously took away from him. I understand how he feels, but what he has to realize is that you can't gain anything through revenge. You have to embrace life, and fight as hard as you can to create from life what you want, regardless of whatever it throws at you. That's how I've lived since my visit to the hospital a few years ago.

Vizor also told Griff, Rodger, and me that there is a place called the Cave of Destiny, which is supposed to contain my secret legacy's past and the lost souls of my ancestors. So we're heading to Pluto next. There's just one tiny problem - the cave is hidden. But the prophecy that Vizor once had I now possess; and with the Prophecy of Wisdom, I am directed toward Vizor's castle.

"Maybe it's a trap," Griff is exploring the possibility of why Vizor left his castle unlocked.

"What could he be trying to pull?" Rodger mulls.

I don't speak at all. The only thing I'm thinking about is the voice that surprised me back at Cairo. It said: 'Because I can see where he is from up here'. Up here? Had It meant the castle? There's only one way to find out.

Inside, the castle is grim and creepy-looking. It looks like something built in medieval times. There are traps set everywhere. We see sliding floorboards that lead to bottomless pits, giant swinging pendulums, and guillotines.

"Are you guys all good?" I look back to see if Rodger and Griff are still following.

"We're fine." Rodger says as Griff avoids a pendulum. "What is this guy trying to accomplish with leaving his castle here?"

"I don't know," I try to think of an explanation, "but whatever it is, why don't we split up to look for an answer? Rodger, you cover the second floor, and I'll cover the top floor."

"Then I'll take the bottom floor." Griff says as he takes off.

"Meet back in front of the castle gates in thirty minutes. Don't be late. C'mon! We've got a castle to explore!" I start moving up the first set of stairs with Rodger. He stops at the second floor as I move on. Just what is the force that called out to me at Cairo? With the trusty Wisdom Prophecy at my side, I proceed to search for what awaits me.

I hurry to the final floor. The place is run-down, smells like no one has visited the castle for millennia, and there is a dark mist on the floor. This is a new feature. I must be getting closer to that force. I start searching for the force under chairs, behind tables, and inside closets. After twenty minutes, I still don't find it. I start feeling antsy since I only have 10 minutes left until I have to report back to the others. Amidst my anxiousness, the Prophecy starts to actually speak to me.

"V, look harder."

"But I searched the entire floor."

"Think V, why do you think there is a dark mist on the floor?"

"Uhh, because that force is here?"

"Think again," it says as if it's toying with me. But then, it occurs to me, –*What if there is something under the smog? Wow, I feel stupid!*

The Prophecy reads my thought and says: "Good job, V. You found it!"

"What exactly did I find?"

"The energy you are looking for. Try blowing away the smog. It may reveal something that will enlighten you."

I blow as hard as I can which reveals a huge symbol that looks like a black phoenix on the floor. It stares at me with dark, purple eyes. I feel myself drawn in, and the Prophecy and I teleport to a mysterious cave! Where to exactly? I have a hunch that we are at the...

"V," the Prophecy is always one step ahead of the game, "look up ahead."

As I look, there is that same dark phoenix in front of me, but this time, it's not a picture. It's real!

"V," the darkness begins to speak, "you've finally found Me!"

"What are You? Why did You call out to me?"

"I am the legendary Dark Spirit. I will aid you in your quest to stop your galaxy's destruction. V, you are destined to save your galaxy. But you cannot do it alone. That is why I am here."

The galaxy? Destroyed? And I have to save it? What is all of this? For all I know, this is just one of the mystery man's tricks. ...Still, it DID say it would be back for me. If that's true, then I do need all of the help I can get. And this dark phoenix is AWESOME. Let's probe a little deeper...

"Whoa, cool! How are You doing that?"

"Doing what?"

"Well...that." I point to Its general direction. "Just being, I guess."

"This is just the start, V. There are far stranger things to come."

That's a cool, yet frightening, thought. "First, before I agree to save anything, what is my legacy, and why is it important?"

"Your legacy is the will of the Solar Prophecies, your first ancestors, and their Creator, God."

"Do You mean...?"

"Yes, V, the God that created the Heavens and the Earth. I guess now I should tell you how I got here. God created Me. V, with light comes darkness. However, darkness doesn't necessarily mean evil. The only way to defeat Vizor and save your galaxy is to use My dark energy with the Solar Prophecies' light energy. Light alone cannot stop Vizor because he plans to use both light and dark as well - his own heart being dark energy, and the Solar Prophecies being light energy. V, I can also be helpful if you ever need more energy to perform certain tasks. Dark energy is different from light energy. Also, I know your ancestors. They are the ones who tried to unite the Earth and create a utopia, but failed."

"How did they fail? And are they here? What utopia?" I have so many questions since no one, specifically my parents, ever bothered to explain any of this to me earlier. Why did they not tell me about this? Was it to protect me from something? This is all coming so suddenly...

"The Unbound Evil..." the spirit murmured, "...a source of ultimate, dark, and evil negative energy. It killed them. However, your ancestors managed to seal away the Unbound Evil when the Earth was first created. You see, V, after the creation of the Earth, there were approximately a hundred thousand people, God, and the Devil. God and the Devil fought over control of Earth. This was known as the Great War. Your ancestors pictured a world for everyone to live in, equally and in tranquility. Ironically, they had to fight the people they were fighting for. Eventually, a treaty was made and the fighting ceased. The Unbound Evil and I were created to look over the Earth as our two Creators would. The Unbound Evil then heard of your ancestor's plans to create a utopia and decided to create Its own universe. It attempted to kill your ancestors who fought a long battle and eventually sealed It away at the cost of their lives. They scattered several stone tablets to help you, the chosen one, completely annihilate the Unbound Evil when It returns again. And It's about to come out of hiding. This is where your ancestors reside. They rest within the walls of this cave. It's best not to disturb them. I hope I gave you some of the answers that you need."

—I don't know. What do you think, Prophecy of Wisdom?

—Well I myself know the Dark Spirit. V, I know this is all so sudden and that you probably don't believe any of this. But we're only trying to help you and your galaxy.

—Well, you really haven't given me a reason to NOT trust you. I just have to believe.

—You are not like most humans...giving these supernatural forces a chance.

—Well everyone deserves at least one.

So after discussing the level of trust I have with the Wisdom

Prophecy, I accept the Dark Spirit, and It becomes one with my body, as that was also apparently meant to be. A strange chill envelops my soul like a river inside of me has been unclogged. After a few seconds the Dark Spirit seems to sift through my body like my own blood. But I still have one question. "Is this the Cave of Destiny?"

"Yes," the Dark Spirit answers. "This is also the place where your ancestors predicted your birth. Thus, a legacy was born. And it was yours, V."

"My birth was significant? You mean my birth marked a major event in history?"

"Yes. After all, you are the one who is supposed to permanently seal away the Unbound Evil when It inevitably returns."

CHAPTER 5

Planet Zapzoid

The Unbound Evil is going to return, and I have to stop It? Can this day get any stranger? First, I find out that Vizor is trying to recreate his world by destroying mine. Then, I figure out I'm chosen to stop an evil as old as time itself. But the good news is that I have help from the Solar Prophecies, the Dark Spirit, and my two friends, Griff and Rodger. Wait a minute, I forgot about Griff and Rodger! It's been a while since we separated. I have to get back to them.

"Dark Spirit, how do we get out of this cave?"

"Look at the picture of the phoenix behind you." When I look, the picture changes. Now it is a picture of Vizor's castle. A blinding light fills the cave. I open my eyes and find I am in front of the castle gates standing next to Griff and Rodger. They look as if they've just seen a ghost, and Griff actually falls onto his butt.

"Where have you been, V? You're late!"

"Hold on, Rodger," Griff says getting on his feet again, "maybe he found something."

"Oh I found something all right. Come on out!" The Dark Spirit exits my body and takes the form of my body; the only difference being that It has purple eyes and a slight purple mist radiating from It.

"Hello." The Dark Spirit waves Its hand. "Pleased to meet you." Griff and Rodger don't seem too pleased because right after the introduction, they both charge at the Dark Spirit. As expected, they go right through it and fall hard to the ground.

"Now, now," the Dark Spirit starts, "is that the way you treat a friend?"

"Friend?" Rodger asks sounding confused. "V, what's going on?"

I tell Rodger and Griff everything. I tell them about the legacy Vizor was talking about, about the Dark Spirit, the Great War, my ancestors, and about the Unbound Evil.

"Sounds like you've got your hands full, huh?"

I sigh and nod.

Griff continues. "Well, whatever happens, V, we'll be right next to you! Right, Rodger?"

"That's right, we're family. And if this Dark Spirit is what It says It is, then together we might actually be able to stand up to Vizor."

"Thanks for giving the Dark Spirit a chance. All right, let's go."

"Wait," Griff says, "where do we go?"

"Wow. That's a good question...Well, since we're looking for the Solar System Prophecies, and we only have one, we better try to find the rest. Vizor mentioned there are five, and if they're the Solar System Prophecies, they should be amongst all of the planets, right?"

"Right. But where exactly do we start?" Rodger asks.

"I can answer that!" the Prophecy of Wisdom reveals itself from behind me.

"AAAAHHHH!" Griff and Rodger turn white at the sight of the floating, talking tablet. "IT TALKS?"

"Pretty cool, huh guys?"

"Sorry." Rodger quickly gets his footing back. "We're just not used to seeing flying talking rocks!"

"I understand. It's all right. Allow me to introduce myself. I am the Prophecy of Wisdom."

"My name is Griff. The policeman there is Rodger. He's our legal guardian."

"A pleasure. Though it's kind of surreal saying that to a rock..."

The Wisdom Prophecy chuckles, as it slightly rocks back and forth.

"So what exactly are we looking for?" Rodger asks the prophecy.

"The four other prophecies - the Prophecy of Speed, which has the power of swiftness, the Prophecy of Power, which has the power of strength, the Prophecy of Chaos, which has the power to balance lightness and darkness, and the Prophecy of Solar, which has the power of heat and light. I'm the Prophecy of Wisdom. I have the power to read other people's thoughts and, as you observed, take them over. I suggest starting your search..."

"But that'll take forever to do," Griff complains. "All of the planets are dispersed throughout the solar system by a pretty good distance."

"That is why," the Prophecy of Wisdom continues, "when you find one of the prophecies, there is a clue on it to help you go to the next destination faster than normal. Look closely."

Griff inspects the prophecy and finds the text. It reads:

A place in the Asteroid Belt, comprised of thousands of north and south poles is where the second Solar Prophecy shall be unlocked. But beware; touch an asteroid after reading this...and you might find yourself a bit shocked.

"What does that mean?" Griff palms the right side of his face. "Prophecy of Wisdom? Anything?"

"I can't read myself," the Prophecy of Wisdom points out. "All I know is that there's text on me. I didn't even know what it was until you read it."

"So what do you guys think we should do?" I ask. "Griff?"

"Well it says if you touch an asteroid, you'll be shocked. I don't know if that's literal or not."

"I guess there's only one way to find out," I look down to the asteroid Vizor's castle sits on. "Dark Spirit, come back into my body again." The Dark Spirit deforms and I absorb It like a sponge.

"Wow!" Griff is impressed.

"I don't even know what to say to that!" Rodger adds.

"I'll jump first. With the Dark Spirit's power, if the asteroid tries to shock me, it'll miss. If I vanish, you three follow, got it?" Griff and Rodger give me a 'thumbs up' and the Prophecy of Wisdom, not having arms, just nods with all its twelve inches of form.

I jump first, and on impact, I disappear. The others follow. Where are we? A place where the Prophecy of Wisdom's text said we'd go. A planet made out of electricity, metal plates, and magnets inside the Asteroid Belt. We are dumped right next to a sign that reads: **"WELCOME TO ZAPZOID"**. With no one else around, I tell the Dark Spirit to stop shielding me with Its power.

"Has anyone ever heard of this place?" I ask.

"Nope," Rodger says nonchalantly.

"Never heard of it," Griff says.

Right after that, we see something that is even stranger than Vizor. We see a little floating magnet with two black dots for eyes. Actually make that two, three, four, ten, a hundred! It's like they're the main inhabitants here. Whoever or whatever they are, they aren't too happy to see us because when they finally stop arriving, they electrocute us, knocking us out completely.

CHAPTER 6
The Prophecy of Speed

Being knocked out is never a good sign, but it's even worse when you get knocked out on first sight. I think those little magnets must've done that for a reason. That reason was still a mystery to me, but I do have an idea. I am the chosen one, right? Also, there is a Solar Prophecy on this planet, right? So, I think they knew I was coming, and when they saw me, they wanted to defend their prophecy. I guess I would do the same if someone tried taking something that powerful from me.

After being knocked out, we are taken to a palace where we all regain consciousness. There, we are face-to-face with Zapzoid's lead ruler. How can I tell? Probably because it is a good fifteen feet tall, is wearing robes and a crown, and is sitting on a massive throne.

"So, you have finally come, V." I was kind of getting used to the fact that objects can talk, so I am not very surprised that this massive magnet just spoke to me.

"How do you know my name? Who, or what, are you?"

"I am Zapzoid's king, Electrox the Third. Now, before you ask any more questions, let me explain that you are here in front of me for a fair trial to determine if you are the chosen one of the Legend of V. You do know what we speak of, yes?"

"Of course, King Electrox."

"Very well. If you are the said chosen one, our planet's prophecy is yours. But if you are not...well then, you won't leave this place, ever. What do you say?"

This would've been hard to think about, but with the Prophecy of Wisdom telling me that it has my back, I proceed to try and show these magnets something that'll prove that I'm the chosen one. Should I show it the Prophecy of Wisdom? No, it might think I stole that. Then it hits me. What about the Dark Spirit? After all, It had chosen me. Also, if this king knew my name and legacy without me even stating it, then it should know about the Dark Spirit.

"I accept the terms."

"Very well." The king nods to his guards. "Guards..." They send bolts of electricity at my friends and me. I try to think of something, but there's no way I can stop the lightning bolts. Just as I think we are about to be fried alive, the bolts pass right through us. Then, my body undergoes an extraterrestrial transformation. My eyes... the insides turn dark purple, the outsides turn red, the front right side of my hair starts to straighten so it covers my right eye, and there is a dark mist coming from my body. It feels like nothing I've ever felt before. I feel like a drop of purple ink that has fallen into a lake of clear water.

"So now do you believe?" the Dark Spirit asks from inside my body. My friends take a few steps back, appearing frightened. I feel my face morphing into something not my own, something they've never seen before. I don't even know how it's happening. I just play along.

"That voice...!" Electrox gasps. "That is the Dark Spirit, yes? Only It chooses whom It infuses with."

"That's right," I announce in my own voice.

"Now," Electrox continues, "a question just to make sure that you are the one, and this doesn't involve painful bolts of lightning. Where did you find the Dark Spirit?"

"The Cave of Destiny." The entire room gasps at my response.

"Then it is true! This boy is the chosen one who will save us from his evil opposite's plan!"

"How do you know about Vizor?"

"That boy has caused trouble here before, but we've driven him off every time."

"Then, may I have the prophecy now?"

"Yes, but first, I must tell you more about the Unbound Evil. You have heard of It, correct?"

"Yes, from the Dark Spirit."

"The evil is a divine force, created by the Devil Itself to watch over the Earth as the Devil would. However, what you probably don't know is that It has the power to possess others' minds."

"Wow," I sound a bit frightened. "Dark Spirit, is this true?"

"I'm afraid so. The Unbound Evil is the evil half of darkness, and I am the good half. We have similar abilities."

This can be a problem in the future. To think that it can toy with another's mind...that's unforgivable. Wait, is that how Vizor controlled my friends? Could those two be working together?

"Thanks for the notice, Electrox."

"Anytime, chosen one." I somehow change back to my normal self again from that scarier looking me. I ask the Dark Spirit about my transformation.

–What did You do to me?

–Sorry for not warning you, but I thought it's what you wanted.

–How did You do that? I thought you could only grant me power, not mix with my soul!

The king's guards lead my friends and me to a secret underground room in the palace. It is a lengthy hall, but it isn't very wide. At the very end, we find the second prophecy tablet, the Prophecy of Speed. It can also talk, like the Prophecy of Wisdom.

"Hey, it's my bro! It's about time those little magnets opened up this basement. It's been closed forever!" the Prophecy of Speed makes its initial grand announcement. "How are you doing these days?"

From first glance, I like this prophecy. It seems more laid back than the Wisdom Prophecy.

"I've been all right, my brother."

"Who are these characters?" the Speed Prophecy questions, "and why is there a dark stench in the air?"

The Prophecy of Wisdom tells it all about us, how the Dark Spirit is here, and that the Unbound Evil is about to return.

"WHAT?" the Prophecy of Speed is shocked. "That Thing's back? We already got rid of It once!"

"Then you can do it again," I interrupt. "But this time, you've got us - Rodger, Griff, and me."

"All right then, I'm going with you guys."

"Nice!" Griff announces. "Now we've only got three prophecies to go."

CHAPTER 7

Mercury Mayhem

The addition of the Prophecy of Speed is going to help us out a lot. For instance, after we obtain the prophecy, we are all able to travel hundreds of miles per hour by running! Not only that, but we can fly while doing so. After we hear all that the Speed Prophecy has to offer, we inspect it to see where the third prophecy might be.

"I think I found the text," I holler to the others. It says:

Go to Mercury, for your next clue is there. How do you do that? You simply ask. But beware! The one who is trying to destroy you will destroy the planet you now stand on...

"Oh no." Rodger looks around, alarmed.

"Let's get out of here!" Griff screams.

"Yes," the Prophecy of Wisdom says, "let's...oh dear, we're too late."

We're all trapped! Electrox's magnet guards have blocked the exit. And something seems different about them. They're radiating an evil force from within. Their eyes are all red. What's worse, they look like they are going to fire lightning bolts at us, for the third time. But they don't. Instead, they just stand there as if they are waiting for someone to tell them to open fire. Then I remember what the Prophecy of Speed's text said:

–The one who is trying to destroy you...

Vizor is the one controlling Electrox's guards! In the midst of this thought, we hear a familiar laugh.

"HAHAHA!" Vizor yells while entering the secret chamber. "How have you guys been?"

"Just fine, until you showed up."

"That's just cold-hearted, Griff. What did I ever do to you? Oh yeah..."

"Cut to the chase," I demand. "Why do you want to destroy Zapzoid?"

"Isn't it obvious, V? It's meant to be. The prophecies say so."

"The prophecies don't state the future. They are things that help us write the future."

"Insolent fool, the prophecies are meant to control the future, for they are made by the God Almighty Himself. Why do think they're called 'prophecies'?'"

"To trick idiots like you into thinking that," I rebut.

"You've put your foot over the line, V. That's bad news for you. Fire!"

The magnets fire lightning at us. Then I remember that the Speed Prophecy can teleport us to the next clue by me just asking it to.

Here goes nothing. "Speed Prophecy, teleport to Mercury!" In a split second, we vanish right out of thin air. We land on Mercury, just like the prophecy said we would. It is greyish-brown, and it is really, really hot. Just like back on Pluto, we are able to survive these extreme conditions.

"Okay, can anyone tell me why Griff, Rodger, and I aren't burning to a crisp right now?"

"Allow me," the Dark Spirit says from inside of me. It exits my body and shows us that purple energy balls are surrounding us. They are invisible, but the Dark Spirit can temporarily make them visible.

"What are these force fields supposed to do?" Rodger asks.

"They are made of dark matter," the Dark Spirit explains. "Ultimately, they block out any harmful particles or features that should try to threaten you. For instance, lack of air. These shields will trap all the oxygen you come across and eliminate everything that isn't breathable. Also, if you command them to, they will become visible and whatever touches the field will be disintegrated immediately. Well, everything that is made of regular matter."

"I like it," Griff says. "But how did You make them appear all of a sudden?"

"It was back on Zapzoid of course. I knew V would try to teleport us to Mercury with the Speed Prophecy's power. I figured that humans need oxygen to breathe. So I secretly made the force fields for you."

"Why did You make them secretly?" I ask.

"I just didn't want Vizor to know."

"Good thinking. Wait...is this what protected us on Pluto as well?"

"You catch on quickly."

Amazing! I didn't know It was protecting us since then.

"That's why we never suffocated or froze! So where do we start looking for the third prophecy?" Griff is anxious for our next mission.

"Why don't we start by exploring the planet?" Rodger suggests.

"Wait!" a voice is barely audible from somewhere. We look around, but aren't able to find anyone or anything. Then I see something in the distance, but it can't be...

"There. It's Electrox!" It looks horrible. Its royal wardrobe is tattered and it looks like it was hit with a nuclear bomb to its face. The metal on it is half-black and rusty. I get a terrible feeling as I remember we left Vizor and his army of mind controlled magnet guards on Zapzoid, just to save ourselves. That was a close call. But we also left Electrox there by itself, defenseless. Wow, I feel horrible! How could we do that?

"What happened to you?" Griff asks.

"Vizor used the Prophecy of Power to control my guards, and destroyed Zapzoid. I was too weak, and I was...outnumbered. Vizor is vicious. He can use any one of the Solar Prophecy's light energy with his own dark energy, and use it to obtain his brainwashing technique. Prophecy of Wisdom, it wasn't your power that allowed him mind control. He somehow has mind control power on his own. You're just his source of fuel."

"WHAT?"

That's one of the only times I've seen the prophecy enraged.

"Everyone beware. Vizor is headed this way with my guards right now to destroy you and carry out his evil plan of bringing back his world."

"How does he have the third prophecy?"

"I'm not sure, V. He is a tricky one. If you have a chance to finish him off, do it!"

As angry as his antics make us all, I feel it is wrong to say that. All Vizor wants is to try and bring back his home world. Sure, his method might not be so friendly, but I understand the rage he's feeling. Is that why Vizor took my family? Did he want to inflict on me the same pain he went through? Most of all, was Vizor actually good hearted once? Can we bring that out in him again? I think I know who's behind this...

"Everyone, good luck. I'm...about to rust.... Please...save my people..." With that, Electrox rusts away and becomes nothing but a heap of scrap metal. It's my fault. I could've saved Electrox. Why didn't I? How can I be so thick-headed?

"What's the matter, V?" Rodger notices me grieving.

"Electrox, we could've saved it..."

"Oh don't beat yourself up over that, V. You saved all of us, didn't you? Electrox wasn't in the room, and there was no way we were going to get to it. Don't wallow over something that you could've never fixed."

"BUT I SHOULDN'T HAVE JUST LEFT IT!" I punch the jagged dirt. "There's always a way to accomplish something."

"You're absolutely right, V," a voice echoes from a distance. "There's a multitude of ways to DESTROY YOU!"

It's Vizor, along with his army of magnets behind him.

I wipe my face of dusty tears. "Don't you ever take a hint?"

"No, especially not from little pests like you."

"That's it, you are going to–"

"V, no!" Rodger interrupts. "Don't do it! Vizor is too powerful. We need a plan."

"Do you honestly think I'll let you plan a futile attempt to stop me from eliminating you? I should've destroyed all of you long ago, especially you, V."

–*Dark Spirit...?*

–Let's do it, V!

"That's quite enough, Vizor," I say in a dark tone.

"S-Since when did your voice...?" Vizor stammers.

"Since we beat you back at your castle," I say. "The one that you so kindly left for us after you vanished."

"Hmph! It doesn't matter if you just hit puberty. Fire!"

The magnets fire electric bolts at us. As they are about to hit us, the bolts move around Griff and Rodgers' force fields. However, for me, the bolts go right through my body. It is as if my body is made of plasma.

"How did my lightning bolts miss you? And why are your eyes purple and red? You are a mere human!"

"Then you have mistaken me, for I have something that your powers could never get you. I have the Dark Spirit."

"IMPOSSIBLE! It should've been destroyed! No matter, I'll just take you out myself."

"Griff, Rodger, and you two." I point to the prophecies. "Help me!"

This is the rematch I was waiting for. This is where I finally teach Vizor a lesson about true power. Or, at least I think I will. He is very strong with the Prophecy of Power. With it, he could hit any surface hard.

"Time to turn up the heat!" Vizor pounds his fists to the ground with enough force to cause an earthquake.

"Whoa!" Griff falls over and starts to roll around aimlessly.

Rodger sticks his Tonfa into the ground to make sure the tremor doesn't shake him.

I use my newfound dark power to fly into the ground, but when I try and locate Vizor's position above me... "Owww!" A surge of magma rises out of the ground and burns my calves and back.

–V, let Me help.

–Thanks...Ah! That stings!

Despite the pain, the scars heal right away. It's like the magma never touched me.

–Still awesome. I've got to get used to that.

–Not the time, V.

–Right.

Griff finds his balance amidst the quake and channels the Speed Prophecy's speed and blows by Vizor with two fists to his chest.

"Nrgh!"

"Having fun, Vizor?"

"Just you wait, you little runt!" Vizor rubs the excess pebbles off his chest.

The spewing magma causes a black cloud to hover over the battlefield. Randomly, lightning bolts try to zap us.

Hold on, lightning is attracted to metal. That means…Hmmm, I've got a plan.

"Chew on this, Vizor." He turns around, anticipating another blow, but instead, I stick my tongue out and wave my hands at him.

"You are a dead man walking, V!" That's Vizor's weakness: his own mentality. He is so blinded by vengeance that he is not able to think clearly. Then it hits me. What if I slowly lead him to the closest volcano? It will most likely kill him. I don't want to do that because I know all the pain he has been through. Vizor isn't such a bad guy. He was just really unlucky with what happened to his home, and he's taking it out on other people. Although, he definitely needs to realize that vengeful thoughts will lead nowhere.

Despite my puny excuse of a taunt, he falls for it. Exactly as planned. Wait for it…

"Grrrr!"

Wait for it…

"You're mine! …Owwww!"

There it is. His hair blades attract all of the lightning in the area. He promptly falls over.

When he comes to, Vizor announces, "You're a lot tougher than I thought. I'll give you the Prophecy of Power because you've satisfied me enough, for now. I've got things to do. Bye-bye!"

–That seemed way too easy. Why would he just give the Prophecy of Power to us?

–I don't know. Stay on guard, V!

"Hey wait...!" I shout. But it's too late. Vizor is gone, and so are the magnets. I return back to normal after the fight. Now, we have three prophecies, and we only need two more to stop Vizor's plan. But I have a feeling that getting the last two prophecies is going to be a challenge unlike anything we've encountered before.

CHAPTER 8

Terra Firma Catastrophe

That encounter with Vizor throws me off pretty badly. Why did he willingly give us the Prophecy of Power? Did he not need it? Is he better off without it? Is it rigged to sabotage us?

"Ouch!" We hear the Prophecy of Power yell. "This really hurts! At this rate, I'll vanish in no time."

The Prophecy of Power is cut in half! I don't know how, but it's missing the half with the inscription to tell us where to find the next prophecy.

"What?" Griff says. "Vanish? Wisdom Prophecy, what's...?"

"Brother!" The Wisdom Prophecy rushes over and sees that it's hurt pretty badly.

"What do we have to do to save it?" Rodger hurries in.

"It's the prophecies' only weakness: separation. If you damage one of the prophecies, like the Power Prophecy, it'll stop working completely."

"That's bad, right?" Rodger asks.

"Nope," the Speed Prophecy clarifies. "It's catastrophic. The solar system will be in turmoil if we don't find Power Prophecy's second half in the next two hours."

"Oh no..." Then I hope we could learn from past events. Maybe the Wisdom Prophecy knows something. "Has something like this ever happened before?"

"Yes. And the last time this did happen, which was when we were first created, we found the other half of the prophecy on Earth."

What a relief! That's the best news I've heard all day. "What are we waiting for? We've only got two hours to find the missing half of the Prophecy of Power. Here, place it in Griff's bag." Rodger reaches for the badly injured Prophecy of Power and gently places it in the bag. "Griff, Rodger, and the two prophecies, ready?"

"Always," Griff answers.

"Of course," Rodger says as he finishes zipping up Griff's bag.

"We'll save our brother!" The two prophecies say in unison.

"Then let's go. Prophecy of Speed, it's time to live up to your name! Help us get there as quickly as possible!"

In an instant Griff, Rodger, and I start flying really fast. However, not even the speed of sound could get us from Mercury back to Earth in less than two hours. We have to move even faster.

"Hey guys," I call to Griff and Rodger, "feel like going faster? Maybe around the speed of light?"

"Why not? The faster the better, right Rodger?"

"Yes, absolutely."

"Then let's do this! Focus your energy on your speed. Don't think, just do." Then, we start to fly so fast it feels like time travel. We make it back to Earth in a few short minutes. This is good, because now we have an hour and fifty minutes to look for the Power Prophecy's bottom half.

"Where did you find the other half of the prophecy last time?" I ask the Prophecy of Wisdom.

"Since this time it is the Power Prophecy...hmm... I am stumped. The other half can be anywhere on this planet."

"How about Egypt?" Griff suggests.

"Why?" Rodger asks.

"To pay a visit to the Sphinx."

"Of course," I ponder. "The Sphinx could have it. Let's start there! If it doesn't have the prophecy's half, it might know something about it. How are you holding up, Power Prophecy?"

"JUST GET THERE AS FAST AS HUMANLY POSSIBLE!" Its voice is so powerful it feels like a bolt of lightning running through my spine.

In a flash, we are all gone. We fly to Egypt and get there almost instantly. We head toward the Sphinx, but there is a security blockade in our way. That's a good sign because it means there is something wrong with the Sphinx. But what exactly are these guys guarding? There's not another soul in this city besides us.

"Why is this area blocked off?" I ask the security guard.

"...Eliminate...chosen...one...." the guard answers in a hypnotic tone.

"Uh-oh," the Speed Prophecy says.

This is probably the work of Vizor, again. It isn't much of a surprise anymore. That's why I have a new plan. I don't bother to pay attention to the guards. If I knock them out, what good would that do?

"Hey guys," I say to my team, "ready to dig?"

"You can't be serious–"

"Wait, Rodger," Griff cuts him off. "V could be on to something."

"Okay," Rodger says begrudgingly. "So what's the plan this time?"

"Well first, I'll tell you what we're NOT going to do, and that's fall into Vizor's trap again. He's trying to dupe us. How many times have we run into the same trap? He thinks we're stupid. So, using the Prophecy of Speed, we'll travel underground and hit Vizor with a surprise attack."

"I like it, V!" Rodger is definitely more enthusiastic and efficient once he's on board with the idea. I immediately start to disappear under the ground. Rodger and Griff follow. We start running underground so fast it's almost like we are human bulldozers. We run for a few minutes until we hear a massive roar coming from above. It's the Sphinx, being controlled by Vizor. It has to be. We run upwards toward the Sphinx. All of us try to run through the Sphinx to get inside of it, but we are blocked out by a physical barrier. Griff, Rodger, and I hit the sand, hard.

Then we see the Sphinx. There is something weird about it but I don't feel an evil presence within. In fact, I don't sense that there is anyone inside the Sphinx. But I do sense that there is some*thing* in the Sphinx. It is a powerful source of energy that the Sphinx is using to its fullest potential. However, it has lost control. The energy inside of it is so great that it is going berserk. It isn't trying to destroy any one thing. It's just going crazy.

"How much time do we have left until catastrophe hits the solar system?" I ask the Wisdom Prophecy.

"A good hour."

"Stand back you guys!" Rodger pulls out his Tonfa from his utility belt. "HIIIYYYAAAA!" He charges with such momentum that when he hits the barrier, it shatters!

"Awesome job, Rodger!" I run toward it and start running up its leg. Apparently, the Speed Prophecy's power has rubbed off onto me because I am quite nimble. Not quite as fast as the speed of sound, but swifter than normal. I get to the head of the Sphinx and find the other half of the Power Prophecy. As soon as I touch it, the missing bottom half disappears. The Sphinx starts crashing down and I jump off. I find Griff who has fallen to the ground. He looks confused and doesn't realize what just hit him.

"Are you okay?" I shake him by the shoulders.

He grasps his head with his right hand. "Yeah...just a little dizzy. What'd you do?"

"I touched the other half of the prophecy and...wait...THE BACK-PACK!" I carefully reach into it, and I find that the Power Prophecy is whole again. I breathe a sign of relief. We officially now have three of the five Solar Prophecies. Mission accomplished.

CHAPTER 9
The Unbound Evil

The third prophecy is finally restored to its former glory, and now the galaxy is safe. But I still feel uneasy. Vizor is still out there, plotting his next evil trap for us. Obtaining the second half of the Prophecy of Power seemed too easy. Vizor wasn't even here. He must be planning an even bigger trap for us. The question is: When will he set his plan in motion? He's been dormant for a while now. However now that I think about it, the Power Prophecy, which was in Vizor's possession, had controlled the Sphinx. It might know something.

"Is it dead?" the Speed Prophecy asks, noticing the Sphinx.

"No," Rodger answers. "It might just be tired because the Prophecy of Power tried to take over its mind. I know that feeling all too well."

"I guess you're right," Griff states. "After all, I know that feeling too."

I don't partake in that conversation because I am with the Sphinx. The only things with me are the Prophecies of Wisdom and Power. I am interrogating the Sphinx to see if it knows of Vizor's whereabouts.

"You're telling me you don't remember *ANYTHING* from Vizor being here?"

"Argh...!" The Sphinx gets up, holding its head in pain. "I'm not sure. It was all just a blur. He might've been here, but I'm not certain. It's as if I've been brainwashed."

"It sounds like Vizor," the Prophecy of Wisdom says.

"I'm not sure. I think there's something else to it."

"V, what do you mean?" the Power Prophecy asks.

"What I mean is that I'm not sure why Vizor brainwashes everyone he sees."

"Well he does want to cover his tracks," the Prophecy of Wisdom says. "But if he is covering his tracks, he must know what he's doing is wrong."

"I guess you're right. Let's get back to focusing on the task at hand, which is locating Vizor." We continue the interrogation.

"Are you sure you don't remember anything about Vizor?" the Power Prophecy asks.

"Well–" The Sphinx is interrupted by its own consciousness. It lets out a massive roar, which causes a dark aura to erupt from its body. It causes all of us to vanish within the veil. Griff, Rodger, the three prophecies, and I end up on what looks like a pharaoh's palace with nothing but sand in sight. Even the Sphinx is gone.

"What kind of trick is this?" Rodger blurts out.

A massive roar follows. It sounds exactly like the Sphinx's roar.

"Guys," Griff says, "I don't think this is a normal pharaoh's palace. Is it possible that roar transported us *inside* the Sphinx?"

"I guess so." I realize at this point that anything and everything is possible. "We've got to find a way out. That roar will only get louder. If we don't get to that dark aura controlling the Sphinx's mind, this place will collapse!"

"So this is what was controlling the Sphinx," Rodger ponders aloud, "not the prophecy."

"My friends..." the Sphinx's voice starts to echo, "I don't have... much longer...arghhh...! You must get to the top of the palace where you will find the source of the dark force controlling me. Beware...the palace is said to be cursed by dark forces. GO! HURRY!"

We don't hesitate. Inside is the most unreal thing I've ever seen. The palace is filled with dark energy fields, making parts of it float. This makes our task more difficult. Not only that, but there are fiends in the palace and I'm pretty sure they are here to destroy us. It takes a long while to get to the top, but as we get to the final door of the palace, a dark mist greets us.

"This must be it," I say as I reach to grasp the doorknob. I take a deep breath and open the door. We are all surprised to see the brightest room in the palace. The color of gold in this room is much more lively than in the other corridors, alleys, and rooms in this place.

"Are you sure we didn't make a wrong turn?" Griff asks.

"No," Rodger says, "we didn't. Look up ahead." About five feet in front of him, there is the biggest picture of a pharaoh I've ever seen. I immediately recognize the pharaoh because of the long, gold name tag on the bottom of the portrait. It is King Tutankhamen.

"So," Rodger starts, "if King Tut's picture is here, then that means this might've been..."

"No," Griff cuts him off. "This definitely *was* King Tutankhamen's palace."

We then hear that the Sphinx is almost taken over completely. Who is controlling it? Right when the Sphinx roars, the portrait in front of us begins to glow. The portrait radiates with a dark aura coming from behind the picture. But this one is different from the Dark Spirit. This dark energy gives off an even more negative tone like a heavy gravitational field. All three of us reach to take down the portrait when the dark aura suddenly speaks!

"That won't be necessary, V."

"What are you, and how do you know my–"

"This is impossible..." the Dark Spirit stutters.

"What is it?" It takes me a second to think what the Dark Spirit can possibly be scared about, but then I remember what It told me the first time we met. "Wait, is this the..."

"Yes, V," the Dark Spirit says, "This is the infamous Unbound Evil." A stream of energy crashes to the floor like a meteor, then it rises as if it was raised from the dead. It rushes past me. I feel as if I have just been punched in the gut. I fall down and the Unbound Evil takes on a new form...me. It takes my exact shape as an empty shell, except for two dark crimson eyes and an evil smirk.

"I'm surprised to see You here...brother," the Unbound Evil announces.

"I was about to say the same thing to You," the Dark Spirit replies.

"Hold on." Griff is flabbergasted. "BROTHER? You two are brothers?"

"You've got some explaining to do," Rodger demands. "Both of You."

"Why don't I just start from the very beginning then, eh?" proclaims the Unbound Evil. "I'm certain that this rip off of Me has explained everything to all of you, but what It probably forgot to mention is the entire story, and Its *real* form."

"What do You mean?" I ask.

"Let me finish, boy. After We were created, We were sent down to Earth to carry out what the Devil and God summoned Us to do, hold the balance of lightness and darkness. If We didn't do so, the Earth would fade away slowly until it was no more. But then, a major accident occurred one night. The 'Dark' Spirit tried to find Me after the sun had set, even though It was forbidden to do so. When It laid Its sight on Me, Its light powers were swapped by darkness. This is where the balance tipped. One of Us had to go to Oblivion, forever. However, it didn't happen. This is why your galaxy is now under Vizor's threat. The balance of lightness and darkness has tipped, and it's all My brother's doing. That is why I'm here, V. I've hunted you and your friends through Vizor and now I have you right where I want you. Enough story time. V, Griff, Rodger, and the 'Dark' Spirit, prepare to meet your maker!"

"Why do You keep putting the words 'Dark Spirit' in finger quotes?" Griff asks.

"Because," the Dark Spirit cuts in, "I was originally the Light Spirit."

CHAPTER 10

Scrap City

"WHAT?" This new information leaves me speechless. The Dark Spirit was actually originally the Light Spirit? This is big news. Not only that, the Unbound Evil is actually controlling Vizor's mind? I knew there was something more to his evil actions. Just as he mind controls others, the Unbound Evil has been controlling him. I wonder if he is aware of it? But I might not have the chance to help Vizor because the Unbound Evil just took the form of my own body and wants to fight Rodger, Griff, and me. We've been through fights like this before, but this one concerns me the most. Is this fight just another distraction, or is it actually an attempt to eliminate the three of us?

The battle begins. We all charge at the Unbound Evil, which was probably not the smartest thing to do. As we get within hitting range, It snaps Its fingers and we are all sent flying back.

"Pathetic," the evil insults. "Is this all you have to offer Me? Maybe this is just a waste of time. I should just put you all out of your misery." It then multiplies by the thousands. In just seconds, there are innumerable fake versions of me in the room.

"Dang it," Rodger says. "What do we do?"

Griff has an idea. He starts toward the fake army.

"What are you thinking?" I yell.

"Trust me," Griff says, "I know what I'm doing. Remember what happens at times like these?"

Then it does occur to me that every time we are in a jam, the prophecies and the Dark Spirit give us strength and help us. I nod and give Griff a thumbs up. Griff holds up his hand. Immediately, our three prophecies and the Dark Spirit begin to revolve around his hand. The Unbound Evil knows what Griff is about to do. It isn't going to let him pull this little stunt. The fake army charges at Griff. As they are in striking range, they get blown back, like we just were.

"Too little, too late," Griff says.

Afterward, Rodger and I start toward the mixture of powerful forces. As we do, we also hold our hands up. We are trying to make chaos, a source of energy when you combine lightness and darkness. We learned from the Prophecy of Wisdom that chaos is a form of energy born of a mixture of different elements. It is apparently one of the most diverse energy sources ever, which is why it's so reliable. The mix is almost complete. The Unbound Evil is becoming desperate. It has one last trick up Its sleeve.

"You honestly think I'll let you complete that chaos mixture?" It says. "Not even in your dreams. For you have underestimated Me. I'm a divine force! You cannot destroy Me that easily." The evil then shoots a ball of darkness into the mix and yells, "Teleportation!"

Our energy field turns into a teleportation field, and we get caught inside it. All three of us are dispersed across the world with one prophecy each, and the Dark Spirit is with me. Where do Griff and Rodger end up? I don't know, but I am in a very familiar place. I transport to my home city, with no one around...at all. It looks a lot different now. It is *completely* destroyed.

I collapse onto hands and knees at the sight of this. My home destroyed. And it's all–IT'S ALL–THE UNBOUND EVIL'S DOING! "I'M GOING TO DESTROY THAT CURSED EVIL IF IT'S THE LAST THING I DO!" I pound my fist to the ground so hard that it echoes before the sound vanishes.

After I get a hold of myself, I realize that the city isn't just destroyed, but buried beneath a huge pile of scrap metal. How did this happen? I go to investigate.

As the Dark Spirit, the Prophecy of Wisdom, and I get closer to the scrap heap that was once my city, I vaguely recognize the junk pile. But I have to be sure that used metal is what I think it is. My hunch is correct. The metal that buried my city isn't just an ordinary pile of junk. It is Zapzoid's remains. The sign that says **"WELCOME TO ZAPZOID"** is still there, but the word Zapzoid is crossed out and replaced with **"SCRAP CITY"**.

"Is ALL of this the work of Vizor, including the disappearance of the people?" I wonder.

"It probably is," the Prophecy of Wisdom answers.

"Why is he doing this? Just what is he trying to prove? Can he really not control himself at all with the Unbound Evil inside of him?"

"It's likely. Remember, V," the Dark Spirit explains, "this is the Unbound Evil we're talking about. If It has the power to create infinite copies of you, how do you think It'll affect one person?"

"I guess..."

There is more I'd like to say but a massive explosion in the middle of the city cuts me off. We don't hesitate. The three of us head toward the center of Scrap City. There are goons everywhere, just like back at King Tut's palace. We manage to evade their assault and successfully make it to the center of the city.

In the center of Scrap City, there is a familiar face that we all had thought was gone: King Electrox the Third!

"No way!" I yell. "Electrox? Is that really you?"

It is silent. It doesn't say a word for a long time. We stare at each other for a while until, eventually, Electrox's eyes glow and shoot an electric bolt at us. We barely dodge it.

"What are you doing?" the Wisdom Prophecy asks.

"I will destroy...chosen one..." Electrox finally says in a possessed voice.

"His mind has been corrupted," the Dark Spirit senses.

"Does that mean we have to knock some sense into it?" I ask.

"Probably," the Prophecy of Wisdom answers. "After all, it worked on your friends, did it not? It should work on Electrox." Then it should also work on Vizor. If only he wasn't so unlucky he would be...

"Eliminate...V." Electrox shoots another bolt at us. We jump but are hit this time.

"Arghhh...!" I yell.

That was no ordinary bolt of lightning. It had a dark feel to it. This is the work of the Unbound Evil, again.

—Just how powerful is this deity? Did It really bring Electrox back from the dead?

—Now you understand It's potential, V, the Dark Spirit invades my thoughts. *The Unbound Evil is divine. It can do anything It wants, even break the laws of nature.*

"How many things does It have to possess?" I say, confused, angry, and frustrated all at the same time. I'm feeling a bit vulnerable. I hate not having Rodger and Griff with me. I have to refocus and gather my inner strength. "This is where I draw the line.... Too many people have been hurt because of You. This ends now! Dark Spirit, mind if we fuse again?"

"Let's do it."

"You stay out of the way," I command the Wisdom Prophecy. "I don't want you to get hurt or snap like your friend, the Prophecy of Power." The Prophecy of Wisdom nods and heads for cover. Then I jump and put my right hand up. The Dark Spirit fuses with my spirit and becomes one with me. Dark V is officially back, with red and purple eyes and all his powers. It is time to battle possessed Electrox. It fires a third bolt at me. I merely widen my eyes and the bolt goes right through me.

"That was weak," I say. "Why don't I show you a real attack now?" I instantly vanish. Electrox is confused. Even with the powers of the Unbound Evil, it can't find me. I then appear behind it and swoop down with extreme swiftness and hit the back of its head.

"Critical error...err...err..." Electrox mutters. Electrox is still trying to destroy us. One hit won't keep it down. It then short-circuits on purpose, not to try and destroy itself. In fact, it has complete control. Still, I merely widen my eyes, and the entire thing goes right through me.

"How...?" Electrox gasps. Its next attack isn't electric at all; it's dark. Electrox's eyes turn dark purple and it fires a dark ball at me, which I widen my eyes for, again. But as they say, third time's a charm. This time, it hits me. I go flying. I almost fall into a pile of sharp metal, which I think would have killed me. Electrox then comes up to me and puts a barrier of electricity around me so I can't move. It's ready to deliver its final blow. I have to think fast. I close my eyes and realize my victory lies inside of Electrox. I feel the need inside my core to get to it. I'm not sure how but I instantly go right through Electrox, without inflicting pain on it at all. But I do hit the core inside of Electrox where the Unbound Evil is hiding. I have won.

"No!" the evil shouts. "This isn't over, chosen one." The Unbound Evil then vanishes, and Electrox falls to the ground. Just what is it that the Unbound Evil wants, and why does It want me out of the picture? Could It be feeling the same pain as Vizor?

CHAPTER 11

"Vizor's" Castle Returns

That was some battle. If it hadn't been for the Dark Spirit, I'd have been done for. But I still can't figure out why the Unbound Evil keeps controlling minds. Does It want the Dark Spirit out of the picture, and It to be the only spirit to fill true darkness in the universe? Its goal still isn't clear to me. Could it be that the Unbound Evil has been through things that we aren't privy to?

"Ugh..." Electrox moans. "V? Is that you?" Electrox is still on the ground, but its curse has been lifted.

"Is that even a question? You just tried to kill me."

"I did? I thought I rusted."

"We all thought so too," the Prophecy of Wisdom says coming out of hiding. "Do you remember anything?"

"I'll explain everything I know. After Zapzoid was destroyed by Vizor, I did rust. However, the Unbound Evil wasn't going to let a power like my electromagnetic force go to waste. It restored my old self, but with a slight twist. It took over my magnet body. I couldn't retaliate. I was too weak. It knew you would go looking for the Sphinx to try and restore the Power Prophecy, so the Unbound Evil duplicated Itself. After the evil separated you and your friends, It took me to my planet's remains to hurt my insides even more. Then, It made an explosion occur to lure you into the center of the city. This is where Its plans backfired. It didn't know you and the Dark Spirit could pull off a trick like that. It was overwhelmed, and that leads us to where we are now."

"Are you assuming this," the Dark Spirit says, "or are you certain these events occurred?"

"I cannot be certain. This all happened while my mind was being controlled. I couldn't possibly remember every single detail. I have a feeling Vizor would know the story though because the two separate Unbound Evil spirits used to control us are the same thing, right?"

That was the best piece of advice Electrox has ever given us. I do think Vizor would know. After all, the Unbound Evil is controlling his mind also. He might know something, but where would we find him? We haven't seen him for a while. More importantly, where are Griff and Rodger?

"Electrox, do you know where my friends are?"

"Unfortunately, no. But I do think they might be with Vizor. Think about it, V. Vizor, I mean, the Unbound Evil inside of Vizor, probably has your friends held as prisoners. I would imagine the evil doesn't want them by your side after what you almost pulled off back at King Tut's palace."

"I guess you're right. Where would Vizor be...?" I wander into deep thought, trying to think where he would be. Sometimes the simplest and most obvious answer is the best. He would normally be at...his castle, near Pluto and the Cave of Destiny.

"That would probably be where he is, V," the Dark Spirit is reading my thoughts again. "Come on, we've got work to do."

"But what about Electrox?"

"I want to stay here. This is all that's left of my planet, and your city. I want to protect it. And maybe, when you return, I'll build something for us to stay in. Eventually, we can rebuild Zapzoid, maybe as a city on Earth."

"That sounds like a good idea," the Prophecy of Wisdom says in an optimistic voice.

"See you around." I wave to Electrox. Time to head off to Pluto. One little problem... How am I going to get there without the Prophecy of Speed?

"Wisdom Prophecy?"

"Yes, V?"

"How do we get to Pluto without the Prophecy of Speed's power?"

"Did I forget to mention something again?" the Wisdom Prophecy murmurs. "Whenever you experience a power of one of the prophecies, it rubs off on you. That's how we got into Electrox so quickly. But you have to truly believe that you can do anything inside your core, beyond your limits. Only then will you tap into the power of the prophecies. That is why very few people can use the Solar Prophecies. If you get separated with me or any of the other prophecies all you have to do is believe you are capable of doing anything that isn't impossible, and our power will manifest within you. That is what the prophecies are all about - never giving up and trusting in your own capabilities no matter what the odds are. What gives us power can ultimately give you power."

That is incredibly reassuring to hear, let alone think. I've never had support like that in my entire life, except from my family... The short amount of time I had them by my side.

–*Could that actually be true?* I wonder. *It's worth a shot, I guess.*

"No," the Prophecy of Wisdom says reading my thought. "You have to believe with all of your heart and soul, otherwise it won't work."

Fine, I'll actually try this time. I close my eyes and look within myself. I see...nothing? How could I see nothing inside myself? What could this mean? I need help! Someone, anyone, HELP! Then I realize what the nothingness inside of me means. I have no inner belief in myself because I've always had to rely on someone else to help me throughout my childhood. I've never really done anything by myself, but that's all about to change. Say hello to the new and improved V!

"Blast off!" I yell.

Instantly, I hurdle past the atmosphere and into outer space, the deep black wonder. I remember that the Dark Spirit's shield is still around me, but it doesn't matter anymore. The way I feel right now, nothing could keep me down. The Dark Spirit, the one prophecy, and I pass by Mars, the Asteroid Belt, Jupiter, Saturn, Uranus, and Neptune. We eventually reach Pluto. Something has changed drastically about Pluto's atmosphere. Remember how Vizor's castle was *next* to Pluto last time. This time, Pluto, in its entirety, looks like Vizor's Empire. There are searchlights everywhere guarding the castle, and you can barely see the ground because of how dark it is.

"W-what...?" the Prophecy of Wisdom stutters. "What happened to Pluto? Where is the Cave of Destiny?"

"You're telling me," I reply.

"What madness is this?" the Dark Spirit asks. "Wasn't Pluto nice and quiet the last time we were here?"

"Supposedly. Is that what I think it is?" The Prophecy of Wisdom is facing a familiar structure: Vizor's castle.

"What...?" I gasp. "How did that get here?"

"Don't ask me," the Dark Spirit says.

"Something doesn't feel right..." the Wisdom Prophecy realizes. "This IS Vizor's castle, but a very powerful force is coming from within, one that I've never felt before."

"Could it be the Unbound Evil?" the Dark Spirit guesses.

"No," the Wisdom Prophecy replies, "It's even stronger."

"Impossible," I rebut. "How can anything be more powerful than something that can counter the chaos element that we tried to create at King Tut's palace?"

"Remember what the Unbound Evil said to us back at Tut's palace?" the Wisdom Prophecy reminds us in a weary voice. "It said that It was made by the Devil."

"Could it really be...?" the Dark Spirit looks toward the castle.

"Only one way to know for certain," I say starting toward the castle. The other two are right behind me. Running through all of the watchtowers is not an easy task because there are guard fiends just about everywhere I look. Eventually, we outmaneuver all the fiends and get to the top of Vizor's castle, which, according to the Prophecy of Wisdom, is where this supreme force is coming from. A massive door stands in front of us, the only obstacle between this all-powerful force and us. We are prepared for the worst.

"I have a feeling," the Dark Spirit says, "we are not going to like what we see when we walk in."

I have a sick feeling about that too. Something is off about all of this. Vizor's castle just happens to be on Pluto when we say it would be, and not only that, but its defenses are up. Could this mean that whatever is in there expects us to come and look for it? Is this really just another trap? Even if it is, bring it on because I feel ready for anything. We open the massive door and walk inside.

Remember how I said I was prepared for the worst? Well it turns out I was wrong because when we walk in, I'm horrified to see two very familiar figures hung by chains from the top of the room: Griff and Rodger.

"V!" Rodger yells out. "Thank goodness, I thought we were finished. Where have you been?"

"I'll explain later," I shout back. "Right now, I've got to set you guys free. Watch out 'cause here I come..."

"That won't be necessary, V," a malicious voice cries out. "Hahaha..." I'd know that cackle anywhere.

"Vizor!" the Prophecy of Wisdom shouts. "Why don't you come out of hiding, we know you're there."

"But he is not here, Wisdom of the Prophecies." The voice cracks again. A black tornado fills the room. Dark energy is abundant, and the Prophecy of Wisdom is right. This force is incredibly powerful. This is way too powerful to be the Unbound Evil. It has to be...the Devil Itself.

The Devil finally reveals Itself. "Ah. So we finally meet, chosen runt."

Yup, this is the Unbound Evil's maker all right. It's a horrifying sight to behold - an angry, fiery demon with a dragon's wings spewing fire in almost every direction.

"What do You want with me and my friends?"

"It's not your friends I'm after," the Devil announces. "My main target is you. I don't want you to obtain all five Solar Prophecies, so My assistant, the Unbound Evil, split the three of you apart, along with the prophecies. It went as planned. You were supposed to arrive here, expecting to save your friends and the other two prophecies. Sadly, that won't be happening, because I have your prophecies right here..." the Devil holds out two stone tablets.

"I'm not scared of You!" I retort.

"Or are you?" the Devil replies condescendingly. "Are you saying you want to fight Me?"

For the first time in my life, I really am not scared of anything. I am finally able to confront danger straight in the eye, even if this one happens to be divine.

"No," I reply. "I already did what I had to do."

"What's that?" It replies with a snicker, mocking me.

"Look behind you."

It does, and finds that my friends and the two prophecies that I had are back with me.

"Who said I didn't want you to have those back? Where's the fun in conquest without a fight? See you around, V and friends." The Devil then vanishes.

"Hmph!" I grunt, proud. "Coward."

"Be careful what you say," Griff warns. "Remember, we barely escaped the Unbound Evil's force. What makes you think you could withstand the Devil Itself?"

CHAPTER 12

Unbound Empire

Nobody tells me what I should or shouldn't do, that's up to me. Devil, I'm not afraid to take You on, or any threat You have waiting for me. After all, I've got all that I need right here with me – my friends, the tablets, and most importantly, my newfound inner strength. It doesn't matter what anyone else thinks I should do. I make my own decisions, and that's final.

Rodger breaks the deep silence lingering in the room. "Now that we're back together, we should leave. This place gives me the creeps."

"I'd be surprised if it didn't," I say as we all walk toward the exit. Or at least I thought we are all walking towards the exit. Griff is staring out the window, and he doesn't seem too comfortable.

"Guys," he says nervously, "you might want to look at this..."

"Why?" questions the Power Prophecy. "Is something...? Oh." We all look out and stare in awe. The scenery has changed completely. It's almost as if we are in the Devil's kingdom, Hell. Peaked rocks and lava lie in every direction we turn, and the heat is nearly unbearable.

"I told you all." The Devil's voice enters the room. "But you still question My authority, especially you, V. Very well. I'll make the lot of you learn to respect My authority!" A massive beast enters the room. It looks like half-eagle, half-dinosaur, and it has one additional, very noticeable extraterrestrial trait - it is on fire.

"What is THAT?" Griff shouts.

"A Cerberus?" I guess. "But that's the guardian 'dog' of Hell so this beast is probably something else. Unless it's been described incorrectly in our books."

"I've got an idea!" Rodger shouts. "Kids, stand back. It could get a little wet in here…" Wet? In Hell? I wonder how he is going to pull this off. Then we all see. He has his filled thermos, but will it be enough?

"Take this!" Rodger shouts. He takes out his rope and covers it in water. It's almost like he is holding a strip of water. With this, Rodger attempts to tame the beast, but it gets more ferocious. Water and fire cover the room. Griff and I exchange worried looks because we both know we don't have much time to get out of the castle before it collapses.

"Rodger," Griff says, "come on. We've got to leave now! The beast's fire won't be extinguished. Let's leave while we can."

"Fine, let's…" Rodger is interrupted by a big:

"RRRRGGGHHHH!" It came from the beast. "YOU SHALL NOT LEAVE. EVEN IF I HAVE TO GO WITH YOU! I AM HERE TO SERVE THE DEVIL AND ALL OF ITS GLORY!"

We need some sort of diversion. But I can't come up with one. All exits are sealed by fire. Is it really hopeless…? There has to be another way.

"There you are." A familiar voice comes from the front door. The sound sends a cold chill down my spine. It is Vizor.

"I thought I'd find you here, V. Finally, I will destroy you!"

"Get in line, Vizor." I say quite calmly which irks him even more. "We're about to die here."

"Of course you are. I am going to–"

"Butt out, Vizor," the Devil's voice awakens again. "*I am going to destroy V. Not you. You don't have what it takes…*"

"SAYS WHO?" Vizor replies in anger. "YOU? YOU DON'T SCARE ME! WHEN I GET MY HANDS ON YOU…"

The Devil is clearly luring Vizor into one of Its mind games, but Vizor is so blinded by his own irate state of mind he can't think straight.

"Calm down, Vizor. Or do you want Me to make you explode?"

"Say that again?" Vizor says in disbelief. That's the first time I've ever heard him talk like that.

"I mean you *are* My puppet," the Devil replies. "I can do WHATEVER I want with you. Whether you like it or not."

Lies! I am not Your puppet, and I'll prove it. Everyone, stand back."

"Why?" I reply. "You could need help and–"

"I SAID GET BACK!"

"'K, geez," I scoot back in awe. I've never seen him so amped up.

This should be interesting. Vizor faces the behemoth with kindling fire in his eyes. The beast starts toward him. Vizor smirks. I can tell he knows exactly what to do. He slides under the beast and takes his grappling hook out of his Afro. He throws the hook and catches one of the beast's legs. Then he scoots back as far as he can and lets his tight grip on the floor loosen. Vizor hurls himself toward its leg. BAM! He hits its ankle with an incredible amount of force and it breaks. The beast cowers in pain. Vizor doesn't waste any time. He immediately grapples to the beast's face and charges toward its forehead. He utterly destroys its head. The beast then slowly melts away, and we all look in disgust as this mighty creature dissolves into nothingness. Vizor has proven his point, or so we think.

The Devil seems unfazed. "Oh, you'll learn the truth soon enough, Vizor. Farewell! I can't say I'll miss you."

"Hmph, You don't scare me and neither does Your power. I'll defeat You. Eventually."

"You just don't get it, do you? I can't be defeated. I'm DIVINE! I must exist for time and space to go on."

"If anything, we need less of You. That's for sure," Vizor mumbles.

"You're so arrogant, but I like that about you. That's why you'll soon see you're nothing but just a pawn in this little chess game of Mine."

"Fat chance," I butt in. I was really sick of hearing the Devil go on and on about how Vizor was under Its control. "Vizor goes by his own way–"

"Butt out, V! This quarrel is for Vizor and Me, so why don't you just leave? You know nothing about Vizor to say ANYTHING about him."

"But we still have so many questions," Griff says.

"And you won't get answers," Vizor replies. "Not yet at least."

"Yeah," the Prophecy of Speed interrupts, "but we–"

"UGH!" the Devil screams. "All of you are annoying. Be gone!"

A dark violet wind fills the room, which is now almost pitch black. I can't see a thing. After the violet storm subsides, we are back outside. Except there is one problem, and it is a life-threatening one. If we don't get off the front steps of the Devil's castle in about five seconds, we are all on the silver platter for the Devil's next meal. In other words, we're about to be fried by a fireball. I remember the incredible power that is within me, and my own will tells me that I can do anything. We all seem to have that moment where bravery overcomes fear because, with a nod, we run right through the fireball without any magical powers to assist us. The power of believing in ourselves is stronger than any power the Devil has over us, and we all know it. Whatever is coming next, we will be ready. We feel empowered.

CHAPTER 13

The Search Continues

I have a strange feeling about the last two prophecies. It's as if they are trying to evade me. We have to find them before Vizor tries to destroy the galaxy. The thought of him rebuilding the Milky Way in his own image... I can't even begin to fathom what that would look like. Ugh! Knowing there's a chance of it happening makes me shiver. We have to do everything in our power to try and find the last two prophecies, Solar and Chaos.

"Wisdom Prophecy, do you have any idea where the last two prophecies might be?"

"Funny you should ask. I was just contemplating the same thing. I might know where they are, but it will be dangerous."

"Isn't there an inscription on the Power Prophecy?" Griff points out. "Might I mention we never looked at that?"

"Oh yeah, come 'ere, you powerhouse." Rodger grabs the Prophecy of Power and starts to read:

The fourth brother is located in the sun. Don't try and go there, it won't be so fun. If you do not heed this warning and try to be brave, you'll find yourself triumphant, but it could be a situation most grave...

"THE NEXT PROPHECY IS IN THE SUN?" the Speed Prophecy bursts out of the backpack.

I smirk at the impossible yet obvious location of the Solar Prophecy. "Calm yourself. What else does it say? Is there a hint on how to get there without burning ourselves?"

"I'm gettin' to it," Rodger continues:

Go there normally, it's like walking on thin ice. Activate your only defense, and you will find yourself sufficed.

"Activate our only defense?" Griff is confused. "How do we do that? Do we disguise ourselves as ice blocks?"

"No," the Power Prophecy finally breaks its silent streak. "I think what it means is that the sun's energy cannot touch us as long as we're on the outside of it."

"Right..." Griff says, "but that still leaves the question on how we'll–"

"The Dark Spirit!" I shout as the idea comes to me. "Its dark matter barriers can destroy the sun's energy on impact."

"That's correct. Still, even if my energy fields destroy the sun's energy, what do you think would happen should my shields touch the sun itself?"

I have to think about that for a second, because the barriers should destroy the sun too. However, I realize something else...

"Nothing will happen, because we touched Mercury, right? Nothing happened when we touched it."

The Dark Spirit smiles. "You passed another test, good job."

"Why do I keep being tested? I mean they're the ones who said I'm the chosen one and all. Do they think I'm incompetent?"

"We just need to keep you on your feet, that's all," the Wisdom Prophecy says. "We do not think negatively of you. We are just trying to help you out for when you need proper judgment most."

"Well, I'd like it if you stopped, please."

"Since you asked so nicely, fine. We trust you."

I am relieved at the Dark Spirit's reply.

I think it's about time we make our trip toward the sun. After all, we've already wasted enough time on chosen one tests, and we haven't been focusing on Vizor very much lately, maybe because he hasn't been targeting us lately. In fact the last encounter we all had with him, he aided in our quest. This really bolstered my thoughts about Vizor. Something about him just isn't very clear to me, and that must be part of his endgame. At times, he supports the Unbound Evil, and other times, he stands up for himself. It is as if what the Devil said is true, and It IS controlling Vizor. At times, Vizor would fight over the Devil's grasp over him, and deal with matters his way. He reminds me of myself sometimes. The *real* Vizor might make a great friend one day. Even if he did take everything away from me, I know better than to do the same thing to him. So now I'm thinking how the Solar Prophecies, Griff, and Rodger could help me free Vizor from Its grasp. But first I have to tell them what's on my mind.

"What are we waiting for?" Rodger interrupts my pondering. "Let's go."

"Hold on guys. There's something on my mind."

"What is it V?" the Speed Prophecy's curious.

"After that encounter with the Devil and Vizor, don't you think there's more to Vizor than meets the eye?"

"What're you saying?" Rodger asks.

"I'm saying that deep down, don't you think Vizor could actually be a nice person? Or alien, or…you know what I mean."

"I know exactly what you're saying," the Dark Spirit announces. "I've also noticed that Vizor's anger and sadness clogs his mind. But occasionally, he forgets whatever he feels anguished about and does something we thought he would never dare to do: help us."

"Wrong," Vizor's voice comes from behind us.

Oh yeah…we're still in Hell, literally.

"I would NEVER help the likes of you."

"Well to tell you the truth, Vizor," Griff says, "you just did back at the castle."

"No," he argues. "I was merely protecting my pride and strength. However since that is done and over with, let's get back to the main topic, shall we? Hand over those prophecies to me, now."

"After helping us back there," the Speed Prophecy cuts in, "you STILL want to destroy our galaxy?"

"Like I told you, Speedy, I'm not trying to assist you. Got that? And I never will. Now, hand those prophecies over to me, or I'll take them from you!"

"Guess you leave me no other option then, Vizor."

"Cute," Vizor replies. "Remember who you're talking to. Ready?"

I'm not sure why he warns me that he wants to fight. And there is something different about him during this fight from the last one on Mercury. He seems to be amusing himself and having the time of his life because he is smiling. I can't believe this, but Vizor is actually smiling for a change. Then something goes horribly wrong.

"You pack quite a punch for a human, V."

"Why, thank you," I reply. "You're not so bad yourself."

"Hmph!" he grunts. "I'm just starting to..."

And this is when the beast is unleashed. "NNRRGHHH!"

"What's going on?" Griff cuts into the battle.

"I'm..." Vizor struggles. This was just like the Sphinx, and I can feel *Its* presence. The worst part is that I can't do a thing about mind control. I can still try though. I dash toward Vizor and jump on him, but when I try impacting his head, I go flying, just like I did in King Tut's palace. It's the Unbound Evil!

"Surprise, surprise!" the Unbound Evil says through Vizor's body - much like the Dark Spirit does through me. "Hahaha! What a turnout. I didn't expect the three of you to see each other again, but it matters not."

"Why do you want Vizor for Yourself?" Rodger asks.

"Who said I'm doing this for Myself?"

"Wait, what?" I am confused. If It doesn't want Vizor, the only other one who would want him is...

"Let Me explain," the Unbound Evil begins. "The Devil wants Vizor, I'm just His servant. My mission is simple. After the destruction of Vizor's galaxy, I was sent to rescue him from his home planet."

Griff stops It at that exact moment. His expression says he can't believe that was actually articulated out of the Unbound Evil's mouth.

"You? You *saved* him? I don't buy it."

"Hmm...?" the evil murmurs, for the first time, in an uncertain tone.

"You wouldn't save Vizor out of generosity. In fact, You wouldn't save Your own evil comrades before Yourself!"

"You're pretty smart for being arrogant, Griff," the evil replies. "Fine, I guess you would figure it out eventually. Vizor is another part of your legacy, V, and he has his own set of prophecies, the Shadow Prophecies."

CHAPTER 14

Below Absolute Zero

'm speechless. How could Vizor have his own set of prophecies? Plus, if he does, why is he - or should I say the Unbound Evil - trying to steal mine? There could be two possible explanations. One, the evil might not want me to have my own prophecies, or two, it has something to do with the light of my prophecies. I'm just waiting for the Unbound Evil to talk more as EVERY villain eventually does to spoil their "master plan".

"I'm not an idiot," the evil continues, "I won't talk. You knowing that Vizor has his own set of prophecies is of no threat to me, or the Devil." –*Hmm...it might actually be a good thing. They can focus on that and not obtain their own prophecies...I shall toy with them.* "I have business to attend to, with Vizor. I'll see you around, if you dare..."

"If we dare what?" Rodger explodes in rage.

But the evil vanishes along with Vizor. In addition to that, the kingdom of Hell, which had temporarily moved to Pluto, also simply vanishes.

There's no more time to waste. "We should get going to the sun," I insist to the crew.

They all agree. Suddenly, the temperature drops immensely. Since Pluto's average temperature is already about -350 degrees Fahrenheit, that's saying something. Imagine dipping below absolute zero, where molecules have no motion. That's what it feels like. As we ponder what could've caused this sudden plummet in temperature, we realize our encounter with Vizor might have been a distraction. This whole time, someone else was at the sun, and I'm guessing It found the fourth prophecy.

"Anyone..." Griff manages, as his teeth are chattering, "know the temperature?"

"Y-yes..." the Dark Spirit announces. "It's impossible to read on a thermometer. It's below -500 degrees Fahrenheit. At least you have your spheres for a little longer."

"Wait." Rodger looks surprised. "A little longer? I thought this shield stops anything."

"It does," the Dark Spirit replies, "but look, the air is so cold that you all feel it already, right? If we don't get to a warmer climate, the cold air will eventually freeze you all in place."

I don't even ask how long we have left because to be honest, I am already a Popsicle. We all run as fast as we can to warm ourselves up. Then we tap into the Prophecy of Speed's power, or at least we try.

"Why isn't it working?" The silence makes me realize the prophecies haven't been talking for a while. But even if they aren't physically present we should still be able to access their power. Something must be limiting their power supply. Is it the temperature? We look back and see that the Prophecies of Wisdom, Speed, and Power are all frozen.

"Now...what?" Rodger barely speaks. He looks as if he's about to faint from the cold.

"We have to believe..." I plead. "We have to run as fast as we can, and fly. It's the will of the prophecies themselves. If we believe we can do anything, we can run as we please. Now believe..."

"It's too cold!" Griff's shout comes out like a whisper. "It's too..." Then we don't hear another word from him.

"Rodger...please," I beg. "Believe."

I turn around and see that he is frozen too. There is no hope for them now. I can't make an artificial sun while it's this cold...or can I? I remember the Prophecy of Wisdom telling me...No, I have to believe in myself. I can't rely on someone - or something - else's power to succeed in life. I have to find the strength and will - and right now, warmth - in myself to do anything.

I focus on warm thoughts and feelings. Ahh...a warm hot cocoa on a cold, winter night. All of my thoughts come from what I had in my childhood and from what support I have now in the present. It may not seem like much, but it's enough. A warm light ignites inside of me as I am on the brink of being frozen in place forever. I feel a sudden urge to overheat. My inner spirit rekindles everything around me and… whooossh! A heat wave flows throughout the planet, and Pluto is back to its original temperature, which is at least sustainable for us while the shields are around Rodger, Griff, and me. The prophecies don't need shields, as long as the temperature isn't beyond extraterrestrial sustainability.

"Someone turn the heater on?" the Prophecy of Power vocalizes.

"Great job, V! Now THAT was a test to remember." I laugh at the Dark Spirit's remark. But this is not a time for joking around. Now is the time to figure out who turned the sun off. The Unbound Evil and Vizor were both here just seconds before it happened so… Who did it?

"Let's go," Griff says as soon as he's thawed out. "I've had enough of this frostbite. I'm going to the Sun NOW!"

We didn't even have time to nod. Griff was so determined that he would've gone by himself. We all dash toward the sky and take off. We're so amped up that we make it to the sun in just a few minutes. But when we get there, there is no Sun. Instead, the real mastermind has taken its place - the Devil.

CHAPTER 15

The Prophecy of Solar

"It was You all along, wasn't it?" I state the obvious.

"Did it really take you all of this time to figure it out? I overestimated you, V. I won't make that mistake again. This is your final curtain call!"

So the Devil actually wants to battle? Now? Why? What does It have now that It didn't have before at Its very own palace? Wait...the Prophecy of Solar!

"No," I respond.

"What? Are you afraid?"

"As much as I would love to make You eat those words, I want that prophecy more. And You WILL give it to me, one way or another..."

"Do you honestly think I will succumb to you, a mere mortal?" It says in a mocking tone. We keep going back and forth like lawyers interrogating a witness.

In the meantime, Griff, Rodger, and the three prophecies aren't talking at all. I see them hiding behind the Devil, waiting for the right moment to snatch the fourth prophecy from It. Call me crazy, but this might just work if I can distract the Devil long enough while It is trying to lure me into a battle. However, the Devil is the Master of Trickery, and It can pull any move, anytime, anywhere. "You have the brains and wisdom of a fly. Why don't you forget about this little piece of your legacy's history, before I make your friend, the Dark Spirit, ancient history."

"What do you mean? You have no control over me or the..."

Then I remember what the Unbound Evil said to us, that the Dark Spirit and Itself were made by the true God and the Devil. This is one of the tricks of the Devil. It has absolutely no control over the Dark Spirit because originally, God, not the Devil, made the "Dark" Spirit.

"Good try," I say. "You're not as devilishly smart as I thought You were." That made It really upset, and when you make something like That upset, it doesn't bode well for anyone.

"YOU LITTLE MISFIT!" the Devil screams. "I will make stalactites of your bones! I can destroy this wretched galaxy MYSELF. In fact, with this prophecy, I can now create a blast that will make any supernova look like a mere dust cloud. NOW PERISH, ALL OF YOU!"

"I think not," a loud, authoritative voice comes from what seemed to be the Heavens. Could it be...? An arrow shoots down from the Heavens and strikes the Devil's right hand, the hand holding the prophecy. It grabs Its wrist in pain. I am shocked; I didn't think the Devil could feel or be hurt. And the arrow isn't quite finished because it comes back around and hits the Devil, again. This time, the Devil goes flying, back to where It came from. Hopefully, It will stay there.

"I still don't think that arrow's done, guys," the Speed Prophecy comments. Then, we take note that the arrow is positioned exactly where the sun once was, and the arrow starts vibrating. This is not a good sign, and I think we all know why...

"Run!" the Solar Prophecy screams. We all fly away from the sun's original spot because that arrow is about to replace it. BBOOOOMM! The massive explosion sends us flying. Coincidently, we land back on Earth.

"Was that...I mean did we... Was that who I think It was?" Griff is a bit shaken up by the impact, but even more so by the events that led to it. But true to his positive nature, he quickly fast forwards to celebration mode and shouts in glee. "Now we have four of the five prophecies!"

"But keep in mind it wasn't exactly easy getting this prophecy. In fact, we obtained the Solar Prophecy due to a miracle by God Himself." I feel even more empowered as the words leave my mouth.

"I also have a feeling getting the last prophecy will be even harder than this one." Rodger says.

"Good inference." The Wisdom Prophecy is eager to find his last brother. "Let's go step-by-step here. Solar, show the back of yourself."

"Why?" it responds.

"So we can see the clue to the next prophecy." It turns around, but what we find is more shocking than the time we first found the Power Prophecy. We find absolutely *nothing*.

"Are you sure this is right, Solar Prophecy?" the Speed Prophecy asks.

"Hey, don't start pointing fingers at me. Why don't you try using your head for once?"

"But we don't have heads..." the Prophecy of Speed replies.

"You know what I mean."

"Instead of arguing like infants," an annoyed Prophecy of Wisdom interrupts, "how about trying to figure out who could have taken the writing off the Solar Prophecy."

"There's only one possible answer," Rodger says.

"He's right." I bolster Rodger's remark. "The Devil!"

"So it took you that long to figure it out..." An ominous voice approaches from behind. We were half right about our hypothesis. What took the writing was *technically* the Devil, but in a different form. The Thing that took the writing is the Unbound Evil.

"Surprised? I'll bet you are."

"Why are You doing this?" the Prophecy of Power asks angrily.

"Why don't you keep your head in check before I take it again?" the evil replies. I could tell the Power Prophecy is not happy to hear that.

"You're only taking the words?" Griff questions.

"Why not?" the evil answers. "If I take the words, you can't find the final prophecy, but I still can."

"Hold on." Rodger stops It. "How?"

"Do you honestly think I will tell you?" It replies. "I'm not your average villain. I don't give away My plans so you can counter them like Vizor does..."

I stop It there. "You think Vizor is a villain? The only reason he's a villain is because he has the likes of You possessing him. Don't tell us HE is the villain. Deep down, he's kind-hearted, and I know it. He's done some good for us before, trying to fight Your tyrannical control over his own mind. Do You know how frustrating that is? Of course You don't because You've never been in a scenario like that, have You? Or have You actually suffered and are like Vizor? It doesn't matter. And giving away plans - YOU gave away YOUR master plan to us as Vizor. Explain that."

"How about I have My dark powers DO IT FOR ME?"

I could tell I am getting into Its head. The Unbound Evil now wants to pick a fight with me. This will be interesting because I have already fought this menace once, unintentionally, on Mercury. But I am not sure how this one is going to play out. I need a...

"Ooof!" I cry in pain as the evil strikes me in my stomach. I cringe like a peasant at the feet of a tyrant begging for mercy. Except I have no intention of surrendering. The evil is definitely not holding any punches back in this brawl, so I figure I should do the same. I think it's time my devilishly handsome dark twin made another appearance.

–*You thinking what I'm thinking?* The Dark Spirit can read my thoughts.

–*I guess great minds think alike,* It thinks back to me.

We start to cross our DNA into each other and become Dark V once again. But this time, the Unbound Evil is not going to let it happen, like the time at King Tut's palace when It stopped Griff's chaos energy creation attempt.

"Not this time, V," the Unbound Evil says. It saw an opening during the alienation process and stopped it. Well, maybe It didn't *stop* it, but It did do something. UGH...! What just happened? Hold on. Where's the Dark Spirit? It's not inside of me!

"Correct, V." Something reads my thoughts, and if It's who I think It is, I am in serious trouble.

"ARGHH!" I throb in pain while floating. Wait...the dark shield is gone! I feel weak...

CHAPTER 16

Dark Dungeon - Extreme V

As I awake from my slumber, I feel a drop of water fall on my nose. I am in a dark, desolate place, and it is not Earth. Outside, there is a starry sky. I am still in space. I can't find the Dark Spirit that is supposed to be within me. The four prophecies are nowhere to be found, and it seems that Griff and Rodger are not in the cells next to me.

"Painful," a deep voice says to me, "isn't it? You shall join Vizor in this little game I'm playing with your galaxy."

"Why...?" I ask, knowing the Unbound Evil is speaking to me. "Why are You doing this to my galaxy?"

To my surprise, It starts to explain. "I need your galaxy cut of the picture, V."

—Yes! It worked. It's finally explaining! I'm really just fine. I've been napping for several hours. I must look pretty weak from having passed out but this was my plan all along. It thinks I'm done for and that I can't understand a word It's saying.

"My endgame really won't benefit the Devil or Vizor at all. I'm starting My own empire under *My* rule, and Mine alone. This will be the greatest empire of all time, and will last an eternity. The plan requires a chaos energy source, the power of both light and dark, which is the reason I need your Solar Prophecies. Also, I wouldn't want anyone else to have the chance to retaliate against Me, so I'll destroy the prophecies' origin and this galaxy. This plan has been in the making ever since your ancestors sealed Me away. There is nothing you can do now, for I have predicted every outcome, and none of them bode well for you or your friends."

I stand straight up from my lousy position.

"Surprise!" I startle the Unbound Evil.

"What?" It shouts in Its normal voice. "Impossible! My trance should've made you fall asleep!"

"Exactly. *Should* have. Where are my friends? Where's the Dark Spirit?"

"I will say no more! TAKE THIS!" It shoots out a dark laser at an unfathomably high speed.

"This is my power!" I shout holding out both hands. I was expecting to deflect the laser completely in the other direction. But that's not what ends up happening. I catch the laser instead, which then gives me an idea. I run toward the Unbound Evil. "TAKE THIS, YOU MONSTER!" I punch the Unbound Evil with both hands and send It flying toward the back wall. I run after It to hit It some more. But now, It is REALLY mad. It does something I didn't even know was possible.

"This is MY power, V!" It transforms into a beast that looks like a dragon with arms and a dark crystal core.

"No way..." There are two ways I can look at this fight. One, it can be what most people would expect, that I have no chance. On the other hand, this could be the greatest victory of human kind. I like the sound of the latter better. This will be the best fight ever!

The assault begins. The Unbound Evil grabs and kicks me to the other end of the dungeon hall. It's hard for me to get up because the knockback effect is too great. I have to take a different approach. If I've learned anything from this adventure, it's that everything has a weak point. That crystal core seems promising...

"Don't even think about it," the beast says.

If I thrash on that core, It should disappear. Is there a way to stall It so I can at least find everyone?

"That is quite enough, You fiend!" A familiar voice emerges. It sounds like the voice we had heard back at the sun. Is it really...?

"What? YOU? Impossible!" the Unbound Fiend says. "You aren't supposed to appear to mere humans!"

"But this boy is not an ordinary human. This boy dares to challenge a divine force by himself. V has shown so many signs of being brave, bold, and trustworthy, as well as a kind human soul. And now, I trust him with this–"

Awesome! Maybe I'm going to get some sort of superpower, or...A rock? Wait, this is no ordinary rock; it's the final prophecy, the Prophecy of Chaos!

"So the Unbound Evil was lying. Is this the real reason why there is no writing on the back of the Solar Prophecy?"

"Yes," the voice answers. "I made the prophecies after all. And I always preserve the final prophecy for the chosen one. You have been told what happens when the chosen one gathers all five prophecies."

"I gain some type of power?"

"Correct, but this power is beyond human understanding. It is a power that cannot be forged by anything except divine force. This power is extreme."

"Extreme V, huh?" I stand in awe. I cannot believe the divine force I have prayed to for years is having a conversation with me. "It sounds awesome, but I don't have the other–" God leaves the scene, and the things I am just about to mention now interrupt me.

"Looking for us?" the Solar Prophecy announces.

"First God..." the Unbound Evil breathes in rage, "AND NOW THE LOT OF YOU! I thought I locked you up with–"

"Tada!" Griff appears. "Where have you been, V? We've been looking for you."

"Wait," the evil stops Griff. "Looking for him? You two are supposed to be locked in chains along with the prophecies!"

"Well it wasn't easy getting out," another voice calls. I would recognize this coarse voice anywhere. Rodger jumps from the air vent above down to the floor. "Your goons were a bit troubling, but do You honestly believe You can contain us, You dark thing 'o nature?"

"He's right," the Speed Prophecy says. "What we believe in is more powerful than what You believe in."

"Give up, Unbound Evil!" the Prophecy of Wisdom threatens.

"You're outnumbered, and outmatched," the Power Prophecy adds.

"If you think V was taking a beating a few seconds ago," the Evil croaks, "THIS WILL MAKE THAT SEEM LIKE A PAT ON THE BACK!" The evil then disappears.

"Where did it go?" the Solar Prophecy's first words are spoken. The dungeon starts to rumble, as if a massive fissure is about to snap it in half.

"Everyone, outside!" I yell. We head for the exit that, according to Rodger, is not that far from our location. We get out just in time, before the prison disintegrates. Well, not quite. It is broken down into bits of dark matter and absorbed by something, but I can't tell what. We look around inspecting the environment we have been sent to since it was hard to tell from the inside. It vaguely looks like the Unbound Empire, like the Devil's castle on Pluto.

"Wait a second..." I start to realize something. "WHERE IS THE DARK SPIRIT?" We all look at each other in utter confusion.

"The Unbound Evil..." The Solar Prophecy realizes, "is absorbing It. V, Griff and Rodger was it...? I know we just met, but we need to stop that fusion before it is–"

"TOO LATE!" The Unbound Evil bursts. Its transformation is then complete with one final explosion that almost sends us flying. It now adds a few extra dragon wings to its previous look, and some blades adjacent to its mouth and core. It now radiates a strong purple aura. "I'm quite surprised the three of you can breathe in space. Oh wait you can't, HAHAHA!" Its expression turns to one of frustration, for Griff, Rodger, and I are breathing just fine. "How are you three standing?"

"The belief in ourselves can drive us far, Unbound Evil, and this is just the beginning," Griff answers.

"Still," the Unbound Evil continues, "it doesn't matter. I will defeat you all, here and now. I'll start with you two." It gives a sinister eye to Griff and Rodger. It shoots out purple vines and snatches them! It now has my two closest friends like batteries in their appropriate slots.

"You..." I mutter, "ARE DEAD!"

"I'm shaking in my invisible boots," the evil says sarcastically. "You have no friends left except those rocks, which I will now make disappear!" It shoots the same purple vines to grab the prophecies, but now they start to glow by my decree.

I close my eyes and take a deep breath to clear my head of all thoughts. Enter, Extreme V!

"THIS IS MY NEW POWER!" I shout. The Prophecies of Wisdom, Speed, Power, Solar, and Chaos channel their energies to me. My eyes glow the color of the sun, and my hair starts to slightly straighten and go berserk, radiating bursts of red and orange. My body gives off immense amounts of energy, heat, and light. It's like I am akin to the sun.

"At least I know you'll be a worthy foe. Come at Me, Extreme V!" And so, the battle begins. The evil fires dark energy blasts and dark matter projectiles to try and stop me. The plan at hand is to gather up energy from the prophecies every second, but here is the tricky part: I have to be careful, for if I am struck by one of the Unbound Evil's attacks, I have to charge up all over again. It takes about a minute to completely recharge myself. When the charging is complete, I have enough energy to cause a solar blast, which will radiate heat, light, and a devastating force upon the Unbound Evil. The battle grows more intense by the second. It hits me and whenever my charge is at its acme, I hit back even harder. This battle is like my life. Whenever life hits me and makes me fall, I get back up and hit it harder.

Here we go; I think I have a good blast charged up now. Wait for it...BOOOOOOOOOOOOOOOMMMM! Yes! It's toast...What?

"Hahahaha! Cute. Is that all you've got?" That blast only weakened It? How am I supposed to truly defeat It? That's the strongest attack I have. Oh great, It's spinning around like a wheel. What's It up to, now? "This calls for plan B." It is now showing me Its hostage, the Dark Spirit.

"V..."

"Dark Spirit?" I widen my eyes. "Is that really You?"

"Heh...So you actually found out about the extreme form that your ancestors wanted you to become. I am proud of you, V."

"Are you hurt? Where are Griff and Rodger?"

"They are still trapped within my relative. V, finish It. I can withstand your blast."

"I've got it!" I say after mulling over an idea. I charge toward the evil and disappear right in front of It.

"Where did you go?" The Unbound Evil looks around. After a few seconds, I reappear with three different beings at my side: Griff, Rodger, and the Dark Spirit. Wait! What's that other thing heading toward the Unbound Evil?

"YOU LIAR!" a voice booms, and since the Unbound Evil is weaker now, It almost goes flying when It is hit.

"Ugh," the evil groans in pain. "WHAT? YOU?"

It is Vizor. I guess he was stuck in the dungeon after all because I did just make the dungeon explode, releasing everyone inside of it.

"You lied to me," Vizor starts. "You promised me my home back, and that the Devil's actions were merely an accident. I won't trust You anymore. I will… RRGH!"

The Unbound Evil goes inside Vizor again. This time, It is showing no mercy on Vizor's body. It completely devours Vizor's true soul and the Unbound Evil has complete control over him.

"This is it, V," Vizor says. He shoots out five whips which enter me and rip the five prophecies' strengths out of me. I return to normal. To add insult to injury, Vizor sends the prophecies flying throughout the galaxy.

"FAREWELL, V AND COMPANY!" Vizor fires a dark laser at the three of us, and that is the last thing I see.

CHAPTER 17

Critical Condition-Zaptropolis

. . . **U**gh, that wasn't fun. Hold on where are we? "Griff? Rodger?" I shout.

No answer.

Wait a minute this place looks familiar. It is the only place where there are electric circuits running through almost every piece of metal. It is Zapzoid.

To my right, I see a familiar figure. "Electrox!" I yell.

"V! Thank goodness you're all right. I thought you would never get out of the condition you were in." Electrox explains how he found Rodger, Griff, and me and how Zapzoid's back in action. After Electrox finished its grand metropolis, Zaptropolis, which now rests over the remains of my old hometown, regular humans started to learn about the existence of the magnet people. They are now allies. Electrox's guards detected a great shake in the Earth's crust not too far from the outskirts of the city. They went to investigate and found us. Apparently, we've been completely out for roughly two days. Who knows what the Unbound Evil could've plotted in that amount of time? I ask Electrox if it knows anything.

"I was going to ask you that same question, V."

I guess that's a no. Great, now all of us are in serious peril.

"Have the others woken up yet?"

"I'm afraid not. Actually, they're in worse condition than you. You might not have been affected as much as the others because you've experienced a power surge before, the power of the prophecies.'

Hold on, the prophecies! "Oh no…"

"Hmm? Something troubling you?"

"Yes! The prophecies are gone."

"WHAT?" It's shocked to hear the news. "They weren't destroyed, were they?"

"No, of course not. They were sent flying throughout the galaxy. I'm afraid we have to find them all over again." As I am about to go on about the climactic duel between the Unbound Evil and me, someone enters in a panic.

"Electrox!" he gasps. "Something remarkable has been discovered! It seems we've found a floating, talking rock."

"Hold on," I butt in. "Does it have text on it?"

"What kind of question is that? It's a rock."

"I'm aware. But if this rock is what I think it is, then you just found one of my friends."

"O…K…?" he replies. "Is he all right, Electrox?"

"I know he speaks like he's living in a fantasy, but he is solemn about this and so am I."

"Fine. Let's go. What's your name?"

"V, what's yours?"

"Melok."

We leave it at that. I roll my wheelchair and follow him to the site of the mysterious rock. To explain my exact condition: I have a minor concussion, a broken leg, two broken ribs, and a noticeable drop in blood pressure. I'm weak, so I don't plan on doing anything crazy. However I really hope this is one of the prophecies, and preferably not the Solar Prophecy or the Chaos Prophecy because they don't have the clues needed to find the other prophecies. When we get to the site, Electrox and I find what we are looking for.

"V?" The Prophecy of Chaos looks concerned. "Is that you? You look different. Did something happen to you in that duel?"

"Yeah, the way I landed on Earth was too much for some of my body to handle. Griff and Rodger are in even worse shape. They still haven't woken up since the fall."

"Sorry to hear that."

"Aside from that," Electrox sounds anxious, "do you know where the other prophecies are?"

"As you saw, my power has left me and, therefore, I cannot sense my brothers anymore. However, I do have an idea. We should all go to the place where the prophecies were created."

"All right, where is this special place?"

"It has been destroyed, but I have a feeling it will make a comeback at an urgent time like this. We need to go to King Tut's original palace."

"Like that's going to be a cake walk, " I mutter. "Don't we have to travel through time for that to work? How would we even time travel? That's not possible. No one can do that."

"Not necessarily," the Prophecy of Chaos says. "We have to visit King Tut himself in the Valley of the Kings."

"Isn't he dead?"

"Supposedly," the Chaos Prophecy replies.

"What do you mean supposedly? He's been dead for many millennia. Or does he also have a connection with me?"

"Correct!" the Chaos Prophecy replies. "I predict that if you go to his tomb, something will be triggered and the locations of my brothers will be known."

"Isn't his tomb cursed?"

"Again, supposedly. If you believe it is cursed, you will be infected, but if you don't, well you get the idea. Think of it like you have every dangerous situation so far. Look at yourself, V; you fought the Unbound Evil, alone. Do you know how much guts that takes? How scary can one tomb be?"

It is right. I shouldn't be scared of one tomb. This is what I have to do to get my friends back. Speaking of friends... "Electrox, let's go pay Griff and Rodger a visit."

"We can't right now. You're friends are in critical condition. If we were to wake them up..."

"Trust me, I know. I have an idea that won't wake them up."

"If you insist." It reluctantly agrees.

Melok, Electrox, the Chaos Prophecy, and I go back to Zaptropolis's hospital, where Griff and Rodger lie on their cots. Electrox was right. Griff and Rodger *are* in pretty bad condition. They look so banged up. We get into the room without waking them.

–*Dark Spirit, are You with me?* I think to myself.

–*Ugh.*

I hear a slight whimper within me. It is!

–*Are You all right?*

–*A little shaken up, but yes, I'm hanging on. Why?*

–*We need to wake these two. If we don't, their condition will only get worse, and they might fall into a coma. Or even worse…*

–*All right, I'll try to heal them. Place your hands on their chests.*

I do as the Dark Spirit instructs, and purple mist coming from the sleeves of my shirt finds its way to the intended targets. Seconds later, I hear them moan.

"V?" Griff starts to move.

"What happened?" Rodger holds his head in pain.

"Electrox found us lying on the ground near this city. We were all beaten up pretty badly. The reason I probably didn't get as injured is that I just subsided from my extreme form."

"Okay." Rodger sits up. "What *is* this city?"

"This is my grand metropolis," Electrox states proudly. "Zaptropolis."

"Speaking of your extreme form, V," Griff continues, "where are the prophecies?"

"One of them, the Prophecy of Chaos, is here with us right now. However, what you two saw Vizor do to the prophecies is true. We have no idea where they are as of right now, but we have an idea who might."

"Who?" Rodger asks. "Who else knows about the prophecies except us three, Electrox, the Devil, God, the Dark Spirit, the Unbound Evil, and Vizor?"

Melok clues them in, "King Tutankhamen of Egypt."

"Umm…" Rodger stares in confusion for two reasons. One, that

King Tut knows about the prophecies; and the other, well... "Just who are you?"

"Melok. I am a resident of San Jose. When this city, Zaptropolis, suddenly appeared, we decided to investigate. During the search for clues on how the city appeared, we found Electrox and formed an alliance with these magnet beings."

"All right so you're a friend. Good to know. Now, how does King Tut know about–?"

Before he could even finish, the Chaos Prophecy steps in to answer his already understood question. "King Tut is the only Egyptian to know about the creation of the prophecies. In fact, the realization of these prophecies is how he mysteriously died at such a young age. The Egyptians had absolutely no affiliation with the Solar Prophecies or V's legacy, but one day, King Tut found himself lost in one of his palace corridors. I led him to our palace because we felt we could trust him with the knowledge of our existence. The prophecies being built under Egypt is a complete coincidence. V's ancestors didn't know Egypt would come to be. When we led King Tut there, his realization of us caused a freak accident in our shrine. Up to that point, we had been cooped up inside that shrine for a few hundred thousand years. That part of the shrine collapsed, and King Tut accidentally died in the midst of it."

"Wow, so that's how he died?"

"However, this is how the curse also came to be," the Prophecy of Chaos continues. "King Tut became very upset that V's legacy happened to kill him. He still hasn't forgiven your ancestors. That is why I didn't want you to know this, but if it means retrieving the prophecies... That is also why my brothers and I didn't want to ever tell you about the temple. We didn't want you to foolishly explore it. He curses everyone who happens to stumble upon his tomb because he doesn't want these other people to meet the same fate he did."

"What do you mean by that?" Melok asks confused. "I thought you said the temple collapsed. How can the same thing happen to other people?"

"Let me finish. The temple that collapsed was merely a part of the entire temple. The actual temple is gigantic. In fact, the Solar Prophecy's temple is larger than most modern day cities."

"I thought the Cave of Destiny was your temple," Griff also seems confused.

"It is one of them. The two temples are linked."

"How?" Rodger asks.

"The two temples are not physically linked. There is a magic room in the temple in Egypt that was created to make travel between the two temples easier. However, the one at the Cave of Destiny was never finished because the Unbound Evil destroyed V's ancestors before it could be completed."

"Where is the temple, if it is so vast?" I ask.

"Right under the sarcophagus of King Tut. Be careful, V. King Tut has been waiting to destroy you for quite some time now. I'm guessing he has been planning his revenge ever since his death."

It had been quite some time since we walked in. But there was still one thing on my mind. "Are you two okay to go?" I ask Rodger and Griff.

"Are you kidding?" Griff responds, alarmingly giddy. "We would never leave you behind. We're all we've got, V. We can't afford to separate. Family sticks together. And that boost you gave us from the Dark Spirit helped us heal quite a bit."

"He's right. It doesn't matter what condition we're in. We've got your back ALL THE WAY to the end, V."

"You guys rule." I hold up the index and middle fingers of my right hand and give them my "V" sign, which also doubles as a peace sign. "Melok, you want to tag along?"

"Absolutely! We can also get some more knowledge about King Tutankhamen and Egypt."

With that, we set off for the lands of Egypt, again. King Tut, prepare yourself!

CHAPTER 18

The Long Lost Egyptian Pharaoh

Rodger, Griff, Melok, Electrox, the Prophecy of Chaos, and I set out to the land of Egypt to infiltrate the Valley of the Kings, and enter King Tutankhamen's tomb. It actually came as a huge shock to me when I heard King Tut had died because of my legacy. This is big news for mankind. I am also glad to see Melok so interested in King Tut. As we are about to go inside the Zaptropolis Airport to travel to Egypt, I get a better idea for faster travel.

"Wait a second." I stop everyone. "We can just fly there ourselves like birds."

"Oh, that's right," Griff recollects. "The prophecies are all about believing you can accomplish anything, and that is what fuels them with their incredible energy."

"I'd heard something relating to this from the Speed Prophecy before," Electrox adds. "However, I didn't think it was actually true. I thought it was a mere myth."

"This is all so fascinating," Melok says excitedly. "It's incredible to know such magic and purity exists in this world. To think that your own mind can set you free...."

"You don't need the prophecies either," I continue. "In fact, I'm confident that you, Electrox, and you, Melok, can tap into your minds and feel the immense speed that Griff, Rodger, and I have already felt."

We all close our eyes and try to set ourselves free. Griff, Rodger, and I accomplish the task of flight easily, but Melok and Electrox are having a harder time.

"You can do it!" Rodger encourages.

"Imagine being one of the first human beings to fly because of free will." Griff adds.

The two eventually get the hang of it and they start to levitate a few feet.

"Wow." Melok's eyes start to water. "This is so cool! I can't wait to tell my friends about this!"

"What are we waiting for?" I say. "Let's go!" With that we finally set off for Egypt.

The landscape is exactly how I remember it. There has been almost no change since our last visit. Unfortunately, like before, all of the people are still missing.

"This is so puzzling. How can all of these people just disappear?"

"I have a feeling the answer lies where we are headed," Electrox responds.

"Good point. Keep watch, you guys."

We take precautions to make sure nothing will go wrong at the Valley of the Kings. Right when we've made sure we have everything for the journey, we hear this:

BBBBBBBOOOOOOOOOOMMMMMMMM!

"What was that?" Melok ducks for cover.

"I think I know. Look over there." I point to the Sphinx and the Great Pyramid of Giza. Everyone looks at each other, trying to think what the worst case can be. It is pretty clear that we conclude the same thing. Without a word, we all rush to where the explosion just occurred.

"Dear God..." Rodger says at the site of the ruin. "The Sphinx... and the pyramid..."

"Ugh."

We hear a voice come from the rubble. It's the Sphinx's head. We charge toward it.

"Are you all right?" the Prophecy of Chaos asks.

"No," the Sphinx replies. "This must be the Unbound Evil's doing. My time is about up. V, Griff, Rodger, stop It, please." With that, the Sphinx loses its nose and the rest of it disintegrates into the sands.

"This has gone far enough," Rodger says angrily.

–What do you think? I privately ask the Dark Spirit.

–It doesn't feel like anyone was here at all, the Dark Spirit responds.

–What does that–?

–This couldn't have been done by either Vizor or the Unbound Evil, the Dark Spirit interrupts.

–Why's that?

–Can you feel it? a different voice cuts in. It's a voice I had never heard before.

–Who are you, and how can you infiltrate my thoughts?

–I am your worst nightmare, V! I am the one and only King Tutankhamen.

–Ugh...just what do you want? I ask. *If you kill me, what will that accomplish? You just want to avenge yourself, right?*

–You show a burning spirit, V, King Tutankhamen continues. *For that, I'll humor you. Come, why don't you?*

In a flash, we all vanish. No, we don't go off the face of the Earth, but we transport to a gate that has a sign, which reads:

Valley of the Kings: King Tutankhamen's tomb ahead

This time, King Tut's voice reaches all of us and says, "If you can somehow manage to survive the labyrinth that is my tomb and reach me, then the ritual will commence."

"Wait, ritual?" Griff is befuddled. "V, what's going on? Why are we in front of King Tut's tomb?"

"Back at the site of the Sphinx, I tried to ask the Dark Spirit if It knew who was responsible for that blast. As we were concluding, King Tut somehow penetrated my thoughts and became a part of our conversation. I asked what he wanted, and now here we are."

"Really?" Griff can hardly believe me. "All right. Let's do this!"

We all head into the tomb and try to find the pharaoh's sarcophagus. The space is filled with gaunt Egyptian servants. Could they be the pharaoh's original servants? After running into a few dozen pitfalls and almost being speared to death multiple times, we FINALLY reach King Tut's sarcophagus. I've read about it in books, but seeing this sarcophagus in real life gives me a whole different perspective on the Valley of the Kings. It's the kind of feeling that makes you feel connected to the past, present, and future all at once. It makes you feel wiser. Even so, I still remember that my life is at stake here, and I can't let my guard down.

"King Tut! Come out of hiding and face me!"

"You're quite arrogant, V. From first glance, I kind of liked you, but your legacy is a different story. And if you are the heir of that wretched legend, you shall fall, just as I did!"

"We'll see, King Tut," the Chaos Prophecy says. "We will see." It sounds like someone, or actually *something*, has an issue about being here.

"What's wrong?" King Tut's spirit is finally revealed - though it is shapeless, like an apparition. "I thought you didn't like me, you piece of Earth!" I'm not sure if that was supposed to insult the Chaos Prophecy or not, but it is pretty upset.

"Shut up! You wouldn't know how I feel right now. Do you really imagine that we intended to kill you from the very start?"

"Well," King Tut replies, "of all of the things that could have happened, unless you can somehow prove that killing me was one big mishap, you will all never leave here!"

In a flash, the exits become sealed, and so do our fates, or so he thinks.

"I can sense incredible power from you."

"As expected of you," I reply. "But it doesn't mean you can stop me from using it."

"On the contrary," the pharaoh resumes, "that's EXACTLY what it means." I start to think about the subject matter and am about to talk to the Dark Spirit, but wait, King Tut can read my thoughts. In that case...

—We should think about running, Dark Spirit.

—Yes...yes we should.

Good, we are both on the same page. Even though King Tut looks shapeless, I can tell he is confused. This is our chance.

"Now!" I shout. I open my eyes and give the pharaoh his royal treatment. Everyone around me, including King Tut, are swept onto their feet, and we go to a point way back in time.

"Ugh! How is this occurring?" the pharaoh screams in rage.

"I have crazy powers also, your highness. Look down."

Below us is a scene where there are five square-like shapes, which I'm guessing are the Solar Prophecies' resting place. I also see a handsome figure walking into the temple being led by a light. It is King Tut himself several millennia ago, alive and well.

CHAPTER 19

The Ancient Form

King Tut opens his eyes in surprise. "What is this?" the young pharaoh asks.

"My resting place," the Chaos Prophecy answers.

Then, the quake starts.

"What's happening? Chaos Prophecy, where are you?"

The structure explodes, taking the pharaoh's body, and his life.

"How do I know this isn't fake?" the apparition of King Tut asks.

"You don't," I reply. "What you believe is up to you."

"That's a lousy response," King Tut retorts.

–*Actually, since we're here…* He makes the time-space bubble pop, and all of us fall onto the remains of the demolished building.

–*V!* The Chaos Prophecy shrieks.

–*Is there a problem? Your tone is a bit concerning.*

–*If we don't fix that time bubble soon, we'll be caught in a time-space paradox and vanish!*

As I try to think about solving our grave dilemma, King Tut interrupts. "V, your legacy ends here. This is where you meet your match. I'll show you the true power of an Egyptian pharaoh."

The duel begins. King Tut starts with a flurry of ancient Egyptian infantries. As they charge, the Prophecy of Chaos and the four of us fight back. Griff is throwing powerful punches, Rodger electrocutes many soldiers with his Taser, and Melok uses a spear he picked up to fend off the soldiers. I, on the other hand, evade everyone, and head straight for the pharaoh himself.

"Stop cowering behind these soldiers. You're not fighting; you're like a puppet master toying with all of us. It's about time I cut those strings. Let us go, or this will get ugly."

"You're right, V, it certainly will," King Tut says. "Just not the way you think. Take this!" Suddenly, all the infantries disintegrate to dust.

"I'm quaking in my boots, pharaoh. What are you going to do, make a sand castle?"

"Actually, that's exactly what I'm going to do."

The ground starts to rise and so do my friends. It's time *I* become the puppeteer, and pull the pharaoh's strings. My eyes burst dark red and purple. The resulting pulse of energy causes the sand to subside.

Rodger then thinks of an idea. "Hey, Tutankhamen!"

The spirit looks in the direction of Rodger's voice.

"What is it? No...wait...what are you doing?" To our surprise, Rodger goes to the pharaoh's actual sarcophagus and points his gun at it.

"If you make another move, your beloved piece of history is ancient history!"

"Are you sure?" King Tut says in a mysterious yet still ominous tone.

Rodger's eyes then go bloodshot. He falls to his knees.

"What's happening? Why am I...tired?"

Then I realize why, and only because I can actually see it happening with the Dark Spirit's assistance. The sarcophagus is draining Rodger of his energy. If this keeps up, he'll die!

"Rodger!" I run to him.

"Don't take another step, V," King Tut warns. "I'll do the same to you!"

I don't stop for two reasons. One is that the Dark Spirit is active inside me. As a result, the curse would probably have no effect on my body. More importantly, some people are just worth dying for. Even if I didn't have the Dark Spirit, I would still keep running.

"Chaos Prophecy! Infuse Rodger with the power of light so his soul will be healthy again!" This is the Chaos Prophecy's mystical power, to fuse light and darkness together. It is a master of both elements.

"You honestly believe I'll let you do that?" King Tut says. "Chaos Prophecy, if you move another inch, your ENTIRE alter building will crumble!"

"Some things are worth more than you could ever comprehend, pharaoh! Rodger's life is one of those, and if you're too stubborn to see it, then you can crawl back into the dark tomb you came from!"

This is the first time I've seen the Chaos Prophecy show strong emotion. To this point, it has acted awfully stoical. I'm happy to see it has a side that shows concern for its companions. It doesn't even know Rodger that well, yet it still wants to cure him of the deadly curse. That says a lot about it. Not many people - or things in this case - have this quality anymore, the quality of showing such great compassion.

–*I wonder if there is a way to trap the spirit. Hmm…* Griff scans the room to see if there is anything there that he can use.

–*How did you trap King Tut earlier?* I ask the Dark Spirit.

–*Time bubble. How is that relevant to what is happening now?*

–*Take a look at Griff.*

The Dark Spirit realizes Griff is searching for something.

–*Hold on.* The Dark Spirit tries to fit the pieces together. *Is he looking for a way to trap the spirit of King Tut?*

–*Yes. Any ideas?*

–*That's a tough one. It's not easy, but do you think I can temporarily enter his body to help him?*

–*Why not?* I say.

I go over to Griff. "Hey, Griff. Why do you look puzzled?" I don't want him to know I already know what he's thinking.

"Do you think there's a way to trap King Tut's spirit?"

"Well…" I am left speechless as a mystery object goes right through Griff's body and out the other side. I look behind me and find that King Tut actually…No…

"HAHAHAHA!" King Tut laughs. "What are you going to do now, hero? Griff is gone as well. You're left without friends. How does it feel to be all alone without any assistance?" I look to where the pharaoh's sarcophagus lies, and find that the Chaos Prophecy and Rodger are both…

dead! Wait, something's not right. I look at them with the Dark Spirit's eyes and notice that they aren't actually dead. The curse makes it *look* like they are dead. What the curse really does is make their spirits immobile. Humans have never realized this. Wait...That means King Tut's curse didn't actually kill anyone, but rather made each of his victims freeze in time. Could that mean...? I've found King Tut's weakness.

"You didn't mean to kill anyone, did you?"

"What do you mean?"

"Don't play dumb. I can see through your little trick of a curse."

"Trick?" King Tut explodes in rage. "What do you mean? This is all real!"

"Or is it?" I look at the spirit with sinister, dark eyes.

"Wha...? How?" He looks stupefied. "Hold on, that power within you isn't any regular force. It is divine. Oh no..."

"Oh yes." the Dark Spirit says from my body. "I am one of the two divine embodiments of chaos made by God Almighty Himself. I am the Dark Spirit."

"You liar! This is all trickery. I know what You're trying to pull."

"Or do you?" I say in my normal voice as I walk toward Rodger.

"Wait." The pharaoh's spirit stutters a bit. "What are you doing?"

"Time to unmask this royal fake!" I touch Rodger with my hand infused with the Dark Spirit, and Its power cancels out the "curse". Rodger awakens.

"V?" is the first thing Rodger says. "What happened?"

"You were immobilized. King Tut's 'curse' isn't real. It just freezes souls..."

"It took you that long to figure out? My spell didn't KILL your friends. Why would I do that to anyone? I don't want them to suffer as I did. All the infected ones have to do is use the ancient form of Egyptian medicine to cure themselves."

He really has no idea. "Pharaoh, this curse isn't what you think it is. You are notorious for claiming many lives with it. The 21st Century doesn't have medicine like your people once did long ago. Your victims - people actually thought they were DEAD!"

King Tut is devastated. As usual, he starts by not believing me. "No, it's all a lie! This is just another mind trick..." At that moment, King Tut remembers the first foreign human to ever visit his tomb many years after he was laid to rest. "Oh, heavens, it isn't a lie. I remember the first encounter. The man was, and still is, thought to be dead. Just like his colleagues said when they were down here for the first time."

King Tut then comes to his senses, and snaps his ghost-like fingers. As a result, Griff and the Chaos Prophecy are free of his clutches.

However, this all seems a bit out of the blue so the Dark Spirit and I penetrate the pharaoh's mind and observe his thoughts. To our surprise, we actually see something that is a legit source of King Tut's memory. We see two archeologists observing the chamber. Suddenly, the same mystery object goes through one of them and he falls to his knees. The archeologist bellows in pain. "The curse is real!" He then falls over, dead.

This is enough. The pharaoh really is feeling despair.

"King Tut," I say in a mellow voice, "are you okay?"

"I can't believe I killed so many people. This is a new level of melancholy."

I've never seen any great ruler be so remorseful. King Tut really cares about those lost lives. So now, all I have to do is get the pharaoh to be our ally.

"Are you upset about the lives you claimed?"

"Yes. V, I'm so sorry I almost claimed your friends and your lives. Is there anything I can do to make up for it?"

The Chaos Prophecy interrupts instantly. "How about we restore the time bubble and return to your tomb?"

"Right," King Tut replies.

The time-space bubble is instantly restored. We return to the pharaoh's present resting chamber with the exits still sealed. But as soon as we gather back at the chamber, Griff notices something significant.

"Melok? Melok! He's gone!"

"Or am I?" He responds in a much more authoritative voice. We eye the sarcophagus, and notice that the massive gold structure is gone!

"This isn't funny, Melok!" Rodger shouts. "Where is the sarcophagus?"

"It's actually right below you," Melok responds still out of view.

"Oh no." King Tut gasps. "I think I know what Melok is up to. He is taking the sarcophagus to the Prophecies' temple's center. There, he can nullify its spiritual connection to Heaven, and my spirit will…"

"It must be the Unbound Evil, again," I assume.

"You'd be surprised," Melok responds. "I'm not under anyone's control. I'm doing this by my own free will."

"WHAT?" King Tut says. "Why would you want to destroy my spirit?"

"You've already killed a handful of people on Earth. The last thing we need is more homicides caused by beings like you. Also, we humans need to study your sarcophagus, and this temple is the key to doing so. The possibilities are endless."

The Chaos Prophecy is skeptical. "If you really are Melok, how do you know about the center of the temple?"

"It is pretty obvious. Carved near the five Solar Prophecies' resting places is a map of the entire temple."

–*Or so he thinks…* the Chaos Prophecy thinks. *I like where this is going.* Melok starts toward the center of the temple.

"Uh, shouldn't we chase after him?"

"Let Melok go, pharaoh," the Chaos Prophecy responds.

–*V, the Dark Spirit says, are you sure we should trust the Chaos Prophecy to this extent?*

–*We should trust it. After all, it is our friend and trust is one of the keys to unlocking true friendship.*

–*I guess you have your way,* the Dark Spirit concludes.

We wait a few minutes, but as we do I think Melok discovers and evades our trap because we hear him say, "It's working, it's working!" At first, we actually think he's trying to dupe us, but a few seconds later, King Tut actually starts to feel pain.

"Rrgh…!" King Tut flinches.

"Wait…what's wrong?" Rodger stutters.

"Melok isn't kidding. He's actually draining my sarcophagus's spiritual connection with Heaven."

Rodger doesn't hesitate. He immediately runs into the heart of the temple, knowing the stakes. He doesn't care if he gets lost or hurt because he wants King Tut and us safe.

"You three get out!" Rodger says to us as he runs. We pretend to agree. Does he really think we're going to let him waltz into that temple by himself? However, we have to act fast because the pharaoh's spirit is diminishing rapidly, and it doesn't look like it could hold on for much longer. I am not about to let one of the most admired spirits in history vanish. I have an idea.

"King Tut, how do you feel? Can you continue?"

"No," King Tut murmurs. "V, Griff, go and retrieve my tomb. It's... too late for me. I guess this is what I deserve after taking so many lives with my curse."

"No," I reply solemnly. "Your spirit will live! If your tomb is off limits, then live within my spirit." King Tut looks with a bit of worry, then smiles.

"Thank you!" King Tut diminishes into particles of light and enters my body. It feels weird, and I smell 5,000 years old. But at least I have saved the pharaoh's spirit. Now to catch Melok!

—Need some help? King Tut asks. *I've roamed this place thousands of times, literally. I can help you navigate through.*

—I'd appreciate it.

His spirit starts to change my eye color to his own when he was alive. His eyes were a dark golden hue, which would still look unique and amazing today. He proceeds to run through the vast temple. Griff and the Chaos Prophecy follow. We all run closer and closer toward the center of the temple. But the closer we get, the more the building starts to shake. We finally find Rodger and Melok in the main chamber. It is definitely the biggest room in this city-sized building. Numerous silver lined columns support this room that looks as if it were designed to contact Heaven. There is a mystical feel to it. The prophecies are about achieving the impossible, and this is no exception.

"Ha!" Melok shouts. "You're too late, Prophecy of Chaos, Griff, and V. The sarcophagus is drained of its connection with Heaven. King Tut's spirit is completely dead, and so is his wretched curse!"

"Fool," I reply in King Tut's voice now flaunting his eyes to the point that Melok can see them.

"What? How is this possible?"

"You just don't get it." I continue in my own voice. "You think killing a human body or soul is a solid way to solve your problems. Well, Griff, Rodger, the Chaos Prophecy, King Tut, and I are here today to explain to you and every human who believes in these doctrines that they are untrue. Even if you physically destroy a human body, you can never take their spirit away from the world. In addition, you say that you have to study the sarcophagus for human advancement. But we know it's for your own selfish ambitions, so that you can be timeless and remembered for your contribution to human knowledge. But if you do destroy King Tut, all you'll really be remembered for is being a coward, a fraud and a traitor. And you still won't be able to research more about Egypt."

"Really?" Melok responds in an ominous, intimidating tone. "And just who will stop me?"

"All the people and spirits that believe what you are doing is wrong. And I've got bad news for you. Some of those beings happen to be Griff, Rodger, the Chaos Prophecy, King Tut, and me. Your 'ambitious' days are finished, Melok."

"Who says what I'm doing is not righteous. I'm merely delivering justice to human kind. All the people lost to King Tut's curse–"

"Let me stop you there," Griff interrupts. "King Tut confessed that he didn't mean to 'kill' anyone. He merely froze them in time. Revenge is never the answer, and even if you are to destroy us all, that doesn't make you any better than King Tut and his curse. In fact, you will be the true murderer of all those people because everyone affected by the pharaoh's curse is not really dead. We can restore them back to their formal selves but we won't be able to do that if you wipe out the one hope of accomplishing that task, King Tut."

"Do you really expect me to believe him?" Melok responds.

It looks like there is no way out of this inevitable brawl.

Then Rodger steps in. "Why would you try to destroy King Tut besides ambition? Is there a real reason you need him completely gone?"

"Fool," Melok responds. "Again, I am doing this for the humans. I don't need him gone, but the rest of the world does so the tomb will be curse free. And it starts with the pharaoh's wretched magic-like ways. The world will be a far better place without the spirits that block the advancement of knowledge. Without them and their curses, humans will have no fear of studying the real world."

"That's just it," I respond. "The *real* world is already in front of you. You shouldn't destroy it in the process of studying it. Melok, you're trying to eliminate a part of nature. You're messing with something that no one should be able to control, not even Him - *I point upward.* He made the world for it to unfold itself, and some things He made to be uncontrollable. The spirits are one of those things. They are meant to be laid to rest, and disrupting those spirits for ANY purpose is really not okay."

"The more we know," Melok parries, "the better. You just don't get the meaning of true strength. Life is never fair, and this is one of those instances. Trust me, King Tut is too much for us humans to handle."

The Prophecy of Chaos interrupts, "Why try to control something you simply can't?"

"Because humans can achieve the impossible. We have to try. That's something you taught me, V."

"But brutally dispatching a spirit is not the way to go. It isn't okay. That comes down to morals, Melok. You are worse than King Tut if you destroy his spirit because you will be the true murderer of those poor frozen souls. Sadly, you don't realize the truth and have selfish motives. So I'll have to teach you another lesson–"

"No!" Rodger solemnly says. "This is why I didn't want you guys to follow me. My plan was self-sacrifice. I was to destroy this place, along with Melok."

"Are you out of your mind?" Griff is shocked. "This is why we did follow you, to make sure you wouldn't do anything crazy. I know you want us safe, but like it or not, we're family and we will make sure you are safe as well."

"And families get through dilemmas like this together," I add. This should change his mind, and if not, then he might just be under the control of...

"It's too late," Rodger responds in the voice that I've heard with trepidation. It *is* here. How could It have taken control of Rodger's mind? Unless...

Oh no! The Unbound Evil *has* been inside Melok this entire time. In fact, when we realized Melok was missing, that's probably the time It left Melok and entered Rodger as well. Did It start off inside King Tut and leave right before he snapped his fingers to free Griff and the Chaos Prophecy? The evil is not as blatant as It has been. It must be trying to make Rodger commit murder by destroying the temple and all of us in the process.

I commit to my hunch. "Why don't you come out and show yourself, Unbound Evil?" I yell and point at Rodger.

"What are you talking about? It's me, Rodger!"

"No it's not." Griff doesn't buy the act either. At first, Melok looks puzzled, but then his eyes widen in fear.

"No! I thought I lost it!"

"You insignificant little traitor!" The evil now corrupts Rodger's body and transforms his eye color into Its own.

"A deal with the dark ruler..." I mutter to myself. "What exactly is going on, Melok? How do you two know each other?"

"Stay out of this, V," the Unbound Evil replies. "I won't tell you anything anymore." It completely separates Itself from Rodger's mind and takes my form again, but in devil-like colors. It hurtles toward Melok and grabs him by the collar. "Now you will do My bidding at My command!" It enters Melok's body and corrupts his soul even more. The Unbound Evil's colors and mentality take him over completely.

"V," Melok starts. "This is true evil!"

He doesn't waste any time. He charges at me headstrong. I try to deflect his assault, but the force is too great for me to withstand. I am thrown back and land on a hard brick wall. Immediately, I start to feel weak.

"What did you do?" I ask.

"You'll find out…when you are turned into mere bones!"

"V!" Griff rushes to my aid.

"Get back! This is my problem Griff. I need you to take Rodger and run far away from here. Don't worry, I'll be right behind you."

"No you won't! V, if I leave you, you could–"

"Die?" I finish his sentence for him. "Maybe, but that's a price worth paying for your safety, Griff. I want Rodger cared for immediately! If you don't go soon, he'll fade away just like me. Would you rather have both of us die, or just one?"

–I can help Rodger, the Dark Spirit thinks out to me. *But I need to become a part of him for a little bit.*

–Okay! But I may also need someone, or something, here for me. Do You think You could be in two places at once?

–Did you forget about me that easily? King Tut says.

–Are you sure? I thought you were hurt.

–I am, but I can still aid you with the ancient Egyptian power that I wield inside me.

I then get an idea I never thought I would ever dare think. If I can intertwine my soul with the Dark Spirit's, then could that mean that I can...? It's worth a shot.

–All right, Dark Spirit. Go to Rodger and help him up.

Without a word, the Dark Spirit leaves me, and drifts toward Rodger. However, I think Melok sees It because he says, "You're mine!" He shoots out whips, much like the ones we saw the Unbound Evil use to disperse the prophecies throughout the solar system, or maybe even the galaxy, and catches the Dark Spirit. Melok then undergoes another transformation. He turns into something that is straight out of a mythology tale. He grows ten feet, gets two pairs of blades on his arms, grows massive muscle mass to the point where his shirt starts to tear, and radiates an unnerving dark aura. "Haha! You've lost! Give in."

"G-Griff..." I stutter, but before I can continue, I close my eyes and reopen as King Tut's eyes. Then, I say in a voice that is a mix of King Tut's and mine, "RUN!"

Griff finally obeys. He grabs Rodger and takes off.

"Chaos Prophecy, go with him in case he needs something."

"All right, V. Come out alive kid, please."

"Don't worry about me." I smile. "I'll be fine, though I wouldn't say the same for you, Melok!"

–Ready, pharaoh?

–Yes, V. Go, ancient Egyptian transformation!

I close my eyes, and I concentrate on my inner soul. There, I see the human form of King Tut - which looks identical to the one we saw earlier in the time bubble. We smack our hands against each other and both dissolve. In the conscious world, I start to transform. My hair glows a faint gold-like, brown, and the two ends of my hair grow to make a "V" shape. My wardrobe changes to a silky, purple robe, several Egyptian necklaces, and old, tattered pants. My eyes then match my hair color - a mix of King Tut's and my eyes. In addition, my eyes and body radiate an ancient magic that immediately grabs Melok's attention.

"Behold," I say in my own voice, "Ancient V!"

CHAPTER 20

Ancient V vs. Unbound Melok

I felt great. I felt like nothing could bring me down, including Melok and his cowardly, fiendish friend who loves to corrupt people's souls. "Impressive, I'll admit," Melok says. "But not as all-mighty as THIS!" He shoots out his tentacle whips, again.

"Is that the best you can do?" I merely flick my wrists and all tentacles are immediately snapped in half. "All-mighty?" I lift an eyebrow. "Come at me, and this time, try."

"Grr..." Melok grumbles. He runs toward me this time, but I move quickly and kick his shin. He falls.

"I'm still waiting for an effort," I mock.

"You little... THING!" He snaps his fingers.

–V, King Tut warns, behind you!

I immediately roundhouse kick backwards and inadvertently kick Griff really hard. As I am about to say "What have I done?" I realize he is tainted by the Unbound Evil also. So, I make sure to kick him in the head, where the source of all brainwashing occurs. The part of the evil then retreats, holding Its metaphoric head grumbling "Ow..." While he is still on the floor, I grab Melok by his shirt collar and yell in his face to make myself perfectly clear. "Stop hiding behind my friends!"

"If you insist." Melok does a back-jump kick on my face and sends me flying. I hit the sarcophagus, and it feels like a lifeless stone. It reminds me of how Melok tried to destroy the pharaoh's soul. Now, he's after me. Bring it on.

"Is that it?" I shoot him a disappointed look.

"Arghh!" Melok sprints so fast I almost don't have time to react. I find a kick coming straight toward me, and I react at the perfect time. Melok is now off balance. This is my chance, but I don't want to destroy him. Melok didn't do anything wrong. The Unbound Evil transformed him into a monster that doesn't care who he hurts, as long as he gets what he wants. The Unbound Evil still makes me sick. I vanish and reappear behind Melok, and firmly grasp the back of his head.

"Take this you hell hound!" I send a surge of energy through Melok's head.

He screams, "AAAARRRGGGGHHHH!" Melok regains his own consciousness, but only for a moment.

"V? Ow. Where am I?"

I start to really feel bad for him. Then, King Tut devises a plan.

–V! There might be a way to separate the two.

–Please, let me hear it. I don't want my friend hurting any longer.

–Remember my sarcophagus? Well, it has the power to connect souls, and to separate them also. It is how I became connected to Heaven. But there is a problem that I believe you already know–

–Yeah, I cut him off in a sad tone. Your sarcophagus's power was recently drained. Why even bring that up unless...Are you going to...?

–I will become the sarcophagus's power source. I am a spirit of Heaven, so I fit the bill for a power source. True, you'll be normal again, but it's all we can do at this point. The Unbound Evil is ruthlessly strong, and this is the only way to separate him from Melok.

–But, that might destroy you.

–And I will have finally paid for making so many people suffer.

I am shocked. King Tut really meant no harm to those people. This goes to show things aren't always exactly as they seem. Our interpretation of history is just that, an interpretation. King Tut isn't such a bad spirit. He means well, and that can drive anyone to achieve their goals. I back away from Melok and slowly start toward the sarcophagus.

"Running already?" he mocks. "What happened to the brave chosen one? I guess someone who doesn't care for his friends now replaces him."

Trust me, I would be thrashing you if I *really* didn't care about my friends. But my friend, right now, wants me to do something for him, and I won't let him down. I stealthily place my hand on the sarcophagus, but the evil sees what we want to carry out and tries to put an end to it. *Tries*.

"No!" Melok's eyes widen. "He plans to make it a de-fusing chamber."

The Unbound Evil thinks to Itself: *I don't need this body. I can extract all of this human's life force. Then, I won't need to be a living parasite anymore. Why have I not thought of this before? Probably because I've never really needed My own body until now.*

I look toward the sarcophagus, and see that the transition for the pharaoh is going well. However...*How come Melok isn't putting a stop to this?* I turn around, and find my answer. The Unbound Evil and Melok are separating, but in the most horrific way possible. The evil is draining Melok's life force!

–*Do you think you can take over from here?* I ask the pharaoh.

–*I'm about done.*

I let go of the sarcophagus, and my ancient form subsides. I have no spirit helping me anymore, except my own, which is all I really need. I rush toward Melok.

"What have You done?"

"Isn't it obvious?" the Unbound Evil says. "I've drained Melok's spirit of all its energy. He is no more."

I would've lost it, but that wouldn't solve anything. Instead, I say, "Oh good, I thought you killed him." I know what the Unbound Evil just told me is a lie. You might physically destroy a person, but it takes so much more to spiritually or mentally destroy him.

"Did you NOT just hear what I said? I destroyed your friend's soul!"

"No, You didn't." It seems the more I reject It, the more irritated It becomes. This can be used to my advantage.

"Are you deaf?" The Unbound Evil stares at me like I have major mental problems that need immediate attention. "Your friend is no longer here!"

"Sure he is. Have You looked in a mirror recently?" That drives It insane.

"YOU LITTLE...!"

The Unbound Evil didn't destroy Melok; rather It now controls his body. But calling the evil a mortal ticks It off since It takes such pride in being divine and has repeated so several times. That is probably the comment that drives It toward rage.

"I'll make you eat your ignorant words!"

The Unbound Evil charges at me. I step to the side, and the Unbound Evil misses me. However, I realize I am not Its target because It doesn't stop. Oh no! Its real target is the sarcophagus!

"King Tut, watch out!" But it is too late. As soon as my warning reaches King Tut, the Unbound Evil smashes the ancient, gold sarcophagus. I can see the pharaoh's spirit, decimated, on the verge of ascending to Heaven. The evil stops on a dime, turns around, and smirks.

"V..." King Tut barely mouths, "good...lu..." He can't finish and immediately falls. The spirit cannot sustain enough energy to remain on Earth. The Unbound Evil and I watch as King Tut ascends to Heaven.

"Yes!" the Unbound Evil rejoices. "The world is King Tut-free! Now, there is one less obstacle for My universal empire to start its reign."

I respond with the words I've been irking the evil with for the past few minutes. "You didn't kill him, You know."

"What will it take to anger you?"

"How about I show you what it takes to make You even angrier than You are now." I hold up both hands. A tiny, faint glow enters the room, and too bad for the Unbound Evil, It doesn't know that it's King Tut. I close my eyes and feel the pharaoh's presence once more. My ancient form is about to make a comeback!

My body explodes with strength, and the pharaoh and I are one spirit once again.

"NO!" The evil is flabbergasted. "I KILLED HIS..."

"Don't you understand? Spirits can NEVER be killed. Besides, he is already dead. So, how do You expect to kill something that's already dead?"

"I can do ANYTHING! You say that nature can't be changed? I AM nature! I run the show, I make the rules, and I am the ruler of the world! I can dispose of this world with the snap of My fingers! Don't you dare threaten My power with your little morals! I can easily change anything in this world as I see fit!"

"No you can't."

"You are this close to–"

"To what? Death? I've heard that one before. Do You know how many lives You've threatened and claimed so far? You aren't nature... You're nature's worst nightmare!"

"I am anything I say I am!" And right now I am..."

"Let me guess, nature? Nothing can be nature, except something that is genuinely natural. God created Earth and nature long ago, and He created it in a perfect way. You are imperfect - a Devil clone - which is unnatural in and of Itself, that is trying to bend the laws of nature and recreate it. IT STOPS HERE, UNBOUND EVIL!"

The fight continues. The Unbound Evil is about to throw a punch, but then It remembers something.

"Little boy," It says in a mysterious, ominous voice, "do you remember what I have inside of Me?"

I think for a moment, and then widen my eyes in surprise. In the midst of all of this, I've forgotten that the Dark Spirit is still inside of the Unbound Evil.

"No..." I see where the evil is going with this, "You're not going to..."

"I will! I will DESTROY the Dark Spirit. It's an enemy to Me and the Devil anyway."

For an instant, I start to consider what I can do to try and free It. But then the Unbound Evil looks angry and frightened. "Where is It? I could've sworn the Dark Spirit was with–"

"You?" A familiar voice finishes the sentence. "Not even in Your dreams, if You even have any, You monster!" It is Melok!

He looks a tad bit different. His eye color is now slightly darker, and he radiates a slim amount of dark energy.

"Are You in there?" the Unbound Evil asks.

"Surprise!" The Dark Spirit is in Melok's body. "Bet You thought You'd seen the last of us."

"Impossible," the Unbound Evil states, "at the very least I killed you, Melok. And You, Dark Spirit, I thought I had You in my grasp."

"Well, you thought wrong." I state the obvious. "Dark Spirit, You raring to go?"

"Just say the word."

"You think you can beat Me?" the evil smirks. "You've been trying for hours, and still nothing."

"Doesn't matter," I say. "I guess you don't know me all that well. I never give up, no matter what the odds. Also, we have something now that we didn't have before."

The Unbound Evil looks intrigued at first, but then realizes what I'm talking about. While this is happening, the Dark Spirit slowly edges behind the Unbound Evil to launch a sneak attack, but the Unbound Evil isn't surprised. It doesn't even say a word, and knocks the Dark Spirit back into the sarcophagus. Wait...the sarcophagus? It's been smashed. Will it still work? Sure enough, the de-fusion happens almost instantly and Melok's body and the Dark Spirit - in Its regular, serpent-like form - pop out of the gold masterpiece. As the Unbound Evil turns around to admire Its work, I hurry toward It. When I'm right behind It, I let out a scream. It whirls and finds a roundhouse kick to Its face. It flies back into the sarcophagus, which couldn't have been better for us. It de-fuses as fast as Melok's body and the Dark Spirit did, then It pops out exactly like the other two. I think we just won.

"This isn't over," the Unbound Evil says. "I'll find a way...somehow."

I go straight up to It and say, "Well when that day comes, we'll be ready and waiting for You."

I grab the Unbound Evil and fling It away. It is over. We won. Well...for now.

CHAPTER 21

The Prophecies' Locations?

It was a LONG battle, but we finally won. The Unbound Evil has left Melok, the pharaoh's spirit is still here, and I'm in one piece. Actually, it has been such a long fight that I completely forgot to ask the pharaoh the question we had come here for in the first place. So after the fighting subsides, I proceed to de-fuse with the pharaoh's spirit, and I am now myself again. Then I ask the question we've been longing to ask: "Pharaoh, do you know where the prophecies are?"

"Oh yes, the Solar Prophecies. No, but I have a feeling who, or what, might. Come, follow me."

I follow the king deeper into the room where we find a glowing tablet. It looks like any ordinary Solar Prophecy would look, but is five times its size. It might be a master tablet.

"This is the place, V."

"Let me have a look." I stare at the apparent black surface of the massive tablet. I then look a little closer and realize a map is starting to appear. At first glance, it seems like a picture of our solar system. Then it transforms into a map that shows the entire Milky Way Galaxy. It shows five dots, one of which is on Earth (the Chaos Prophecy). How am I ever going to assemble the other prophecies before Vizor destroys the galaxy with the power he has received from the prophecies themselves?

"Is this a joke?"

"I'm afraid not, V. The prophecies, according to this tablet, are dispersed all across the galaxy."

As I try to devise a way to harvest the prophecies, the tablet's surface transforms once more. This time, it transforms into something I've seen before: the phoenix that introduced me to the Dark Spirit.

"Is that the Cave of Destiny?"

"Cave of Destiny?" The pharaoh is intrigued.

Oh right, I forget who I'm talking to. I am certain that I'm looking at the Cave of Destiny. No other cave I've seen looks like it. "I think this means I missed something when I first went to the Cave of Destiny. I think it means the true answer lies there."

"What is this Cave of Destiny?" the pharaoh asks.

"Very likely, it is the Solar Prophecies' spare hideout. It's where I met the Dark Spirit."

"Really?" King Tut's eyes widen.

"Well, go forth, V. I wish you the best of luck."

"You're not coming?"

"After today, I need to replenish my strength."

"Reasonable. Well, if you change your mind, I'm pretty sure you'll be able to locate me easily."

"Thank you, V, I'll mull it over."

I wave good-bye and run out of the building, back into King Tut's main burial chamber. I stop to take a look around to make sure everything is where it should be. The sarcophagus is there, the text on the walls is still there, and the body is still there. Wait...a body? I run over to see who it is. It looks like Melok.

"Wasn't he back at the prophecies' chamber?"

Then I notice the body begin to move. Is it really him? I brace myself for the worst.

"Ugh..." Melok groans in his own voice while holding his head. "V...? What happened?"

"Good to see you too, Melok."

"Did we defeat King Tut?"

"It's a long story." I start to explain the turn of events that has occurred, like how the Unbound Evil possessed him, how he tried to destroy the sarcophagus and King Tut, and how to find the prophecies again.

"Are you serious?" Melok is finding this hard to swallow.

"I know this all sounds inconceivable, but it really happened." I still have a question for Melok. "How did you get up here? And what happened to the Unbound Evil?"

"I'm not sure how I got up here, and I don't know exactly where the Unbound Evil went. But It did say something about taking care of something–"

At that moment, he is cut off and the chamber starts to tremble.

"Melok, run!" We dash outside and finally see the shining sun. Its radiant warmth empowers me. It's good to finally feel the warm heat again. However, we also see an old rival.

"Vizor?" I look in surprise.

He turns around and sighs. "Must I run into you EVERYWHERE I go?"

What is he doing here? The burial site of the pharaoh is now on the brink of complete obliteration.

"Why is it still trembling?" I try to shout over the immense quake. "Vizor, are you doing this?"

"Are you kidding? I can't do something like this!" Then, I think of a likely candidate. Oh no, if it is who I think it is, that battle might not be over yet. Just then, the entire shrine collapses, taking everything inside with it. But from the rubble, King Tut's sarcophagus rises, radiating a strong, dark, and evil force. Beside it is the Unbound Evil, who now has Its own human form. It has long hair that looks gelled to the side to cover Its left eye, a radiation of an ominous, dark aura, dark purple eyes, and that evil smirk right across Its face - much like Vizor had before.

"What are You up to now?" I ask.

"Having fun doing THIS!"

The evil is furious. It uses a tone I've never heard It use. It shows King Tut's spirit, once more, in what appears to be very faint shackles.

"V..." King Tut sounds awfully weak. "Defeat It..."

King Tut falls to the side and disintegrates into a pile of yellow energy spheres and forcefully enters the Unbound Evil's soul.

"I've given you far too many chances." The evil explodes with rage. "Vizor, you're not much help either, you insignificant little traitor! Why would you help V?"

"I am not helping him." Vizor firmly responds. "I'm helping myself get away from You! I know You're only using me to build Your own galactic empire. Not only that, You're using V's planet to do it."

"But don't you want to see your family again?" the evil tempts.

"What's done is done," Vizor says. "What happened to my family can't be reversed. You should know, you took them from me!"

"What if I told you they're with me, right here? In my palm." He holds out his hand, which glows a purple flame to portray imagery. What follows startles me: not only does the Unbound Evil show Vizor's family, It shows mine as well.

"Mom! Dad!" Vizor shouts.

"Vizor," his mom starts to cry, "help us."

"Where's X?" Vizor sounds worried.

"Big bro?" A smaller version of Vizor appears in the flame. He looks exactly like him, but his hair is not curly like Vizor's. Instead, his hair is straight and black as the night. "What's taking you so long to save us?"

"I didn't..." Vizor tries to explain, but then, his family disappears.

All that is left now is my family.

"Mom, Dad, Z, D!" I scream in sad longing. "What has the evil done to you?"

"You can do it, V..." They all smile and fade away.

"How precious..."

The Unbound Evil's sarcasm is starting to get on my nerves.

"I can't wait to crush them the second I see them! BWAHAHAHA-HAHA! But first, I must eliminate you!"

"Vizor!"

"Who? Oh, you mean Me in a shell..."

I look to my left and find Vizor struggling to keep the Unbound Evil out of his body. This time, Vizor is so irked by the Unbound Evil, he finally holds his own.

"Enough!" He throws his arms out and the dark aura lifts from his body.

"What? You're My puppet, My plaything. I say what you do!"

"Not anymore, You hellhound. If it means helping V, so be it. At least I'll stop Your 'master' plan. Are you ready, V?"

"Absolutely! I'm always ready, Vizor."

"How heart-warming."

Again, the annoying sarcasm. "Two distant souls combining to take down the bad guy, eh? Well here is MY distant soul!"

We remember that the pharaoh's soul is a part of It now. This is bad. It transforms into exactly what I did back at the prophecies' chamber. Enter, the Ancient Evil.

"Now...PERISH BY MY HANDS, MORTALS!"

Vizor and I are ready. Vizor pulls out his grappling hook from his Afro. Wait, I don't have anything like that. On second thought, I do - my unbreakable spirit, which is stronger than any weapon. Most people don't understand that everyone has one. I just recently realized it and I think Vizor understands too, which is why I feel comfortable around him now...when he's not possessed.

The battle starts with a series of powerful blows. Vizor tries to grab the evil with his hook, but It gets away. I try to pin It down, but the Ancient Evil is a master of escape and disguise. After all, It is akin to the Devil Itself.

"Nothing's working!" Vizor complains. "How about...THIS?" What Vizor does surprises me yet again. He takes down the upside down V shaped figure in his hair and uses them as twin blades! "YOU'RE MINE!" He throws one sword toward the Unbound Evil to distract It while he wields the other blade and volleys toward It.

"Come now, Vizor," the evil says ominously. "Come now!"

Vizor then stops in his tracks, completely stationary. "W-What...?" he stutters. "How?"

The evil doesn't immediately answer. All It does is walk toward Vizor and takes his blade. "I have no use for you anymore."

The evil wants to kill him.

"No...!" I run toward the evil. "DON'T!"

"YOU'VE ALL BE A THORN IN MY SIDE FOR LONG ENOUGH!" the Evil screams. "Perish by my hands, Vizor!"

A gunshot fires to my left and hits the Ancient Evil's hand, causing It to drop the blade. "Ow! What ignorant fool dares shoot at Me, a divine force?"

I turn around and find Rodger, radiating a dark aura from the Dark Spirit that is powering his body.

"You don't lay a finger on him, ya hear?" Rodger says to the evil. "He's with us now!"

"I keep telling you," Vizor attempts to correct Rodger, "I just don't want the Unbound, or right now Ancient, Evil getting in my way. I still don't like you!"

"Sure..." Griff enters the scene. "Come on, you like us."

"I DON'T CARE WHO LIKES WHO, I HATE ALL OF YOU!" The evil explodes once more. "I will destroy all of you here! *Actually...*" It calls forth a dark force to heal Its hand. "V, Rodger, and Griff," It continues in a tone that doesn't appeal to any of us, "do you know why all of the people here are gone?"

"Let me guess," I say. "You took them, and You're going to use them to somehow destroy us? You're too predictable."

"Wrong," the evil corrects. "I am going to use them, but not to destroy you."

"Hold on," Melok cuts It off. "I thought You wanted all of us gone."

"It wouldn't be fitting to do it here. Trust me, it would seem way too pathetic."

"This coming from the Thing who hides behind everything at all costs, just so It doesn't have to have blood on Its hands," Vizor says.

"I couldn't care the slightest what you think of Me. This way, I can be in multiple places at once! Come out, My pets."

We now see what that trembling was. It was the coming of all of the people of Egypt.

"See your corpses later. HAHAHA!"

The people slowly start to come out of King Tut's resting chamber. Dozens, soon hundreds, and eventually, several thousands.

I look toward Vizor.

"What do we…?"

But he's gone.

"Gee, what a friend."

"Remember," Griff corrects me. "He isn't really our…"

"Does it look like I care at all right now?" I point toward the chamber. "There are thousands of people just waiting to murder us!" I also notice something else. "Where's the Chaos Prophecy?"

Griff appears stunned. He looks around, finds nothing, and says, "Uh-oh. Vizor or the evil took it!"

"Well…shoot. Oh well, play with the cards you're dealt, right? Let's get out of here!"

We start to dash in the opposite direction of the tomb, but…

"We're trapped!" Melok says from right behind us.

"Brace yourselves, guys," I say. "This might get ugly. We have to… There is no other choice. If these guys won't let us through, then we're going to have to barge through!"

We start to shake off a few of the possessed Egyptians. Griff is punching them down; Melok is using one person like a battering ram to mow anyone in his path; Rodger is using his whip to throw people out of the little circle we are fighting in; and I keep axe kicking everyone into the ground. However, our efforts aren't making any progress. The Egyptians just keep coming by the dozens out of the chamber.

"How many more are we going to fight?" Griff asks.

I think about that for a little bit. Then, Rodger notices the look in the possessed people's eyes. It doesn't seem right to him, or should I say, to the Dark Spirit.

"Guys!" The Dark Spirit uses Rodger's body to speak in Its voice. "These people are possessed by the Chaos Prophecy!"

"What?" Melok shouts over the groans of the zombie-like people. "Why would the Chaos Prophecy ever do that?"

"I don't know," the Dark Spirit replies. "But that doesn't matter now. The force that possesses the Egyptians is definitely a chaos mixture."

"That means the Chaos Prophecy must be inside the tomb of King Tut!" I shout.

Griff tries to eye the tomb that the Unbound Evil left behind. He finds it radiates a purple glow.

"Guys, there's the tomb!"

"Perfect! Melok, can you lend me a hand...or should I say battering ram?"

"Sure thing, V."

We dash through the crowd of mindless, purple-eyed shells with a commanding force. We reach the tomb of King Tut, but when we try to open it, the tomb won't budge.

"Great," I flip my arms in the air from disappointment. "Guess the evil isn't so predictable this time around."

"It hasn't been tricky, at all?" Melok sounds concerned.

"It's been mostly predictable throughout this adventure so far. Why does that bother you?"

"I'd watch your back," Melok warns. "The Devil, even Its disciple, is not to be taken lightly. It must have a master plan. I have a feeling It's setting you up. It takes more than just a strong will to take on the Devil. Trust me, I know. Unfortunately, the real world is influenced by the Devil a lot, and It is unpredictable. Sadly, most people are easily seduced, which is a great sin."

"Trust me, I know how merciless the Devil and the real world can be." I think of my family, and wonder why the Unbound Evil would even give me hope that they are alive. It's probably just planning to get my hopes up, and then crush them to expose how weak I am without others. Well, here's my response to that: Unbound Evil, You're a coward, the prince of them; and I'm never alone, like it or not. I have your biggest fear by my side the whole time. In fact, It's with me right now; maybe not physically, but mentally, spiritually, and morally. "Let's get this sarcophagus open."

"That's not exactly physically possible..." Melok responds.

"Key word in that being 'physically'. We need the Dark Spirit for this to work. That's our best chance. We have to go back to Rodger and transfer the Dark Spirit back to my body. I have an idea," I say after thinking this through. "You stay here and make sure the sarcophagus doesn't go anywhere 'cause who knows what can happen to that thing if we take our eyes off it. I'll go to Rodger and get back the Dark Spirit. He should have enough strength to sustain his consciousness."

"If you say so," Melok agrees, leaning his right arm on the sarcophagus.

I fight past the ghouls, again, and reach Rodger and Griff, who are still trying to fight them off.

"Rodger!" I shout over the ghouls' groans. "I need the Dark Spirit back to open the sarcophagus!"

"Why won't it open?"

"The Unbound Evil sealed it. It's not messing around anymore."

Rodger finds this a little odd at first because the Unbound Evil has not done anything this smart in, well, ever, but then he starts to understand where the evil is going with this.

"All right. Here!" As he continuously throws people out of the little fighting circle we have established, he places his hand on my back. The Dark Spirit crawls up his arm and into my body. I start conversing with It immediately.

—You know what to do, right? I assume It's reading my thoughts.

—Never gets old, does it? It responds.

We both know Dark V is the way to go. Separate, we're both pretty strong, but combined we're virtually unstoppable. My eyes start to undergo the purple-red transformation. Our energies combine, and Dark V rises again!

"Let's go," I say in the deep tone of my dark side. I run so fast toward the sarcophagus that I start to lift off the ground a little bit. My speed scatters a few hundred people, making Rodger's and Griff's job that much easier.

"'K, I'm back," I say to Melok.

His eyes widen, probably because he's never seen me like this.

"Who is...?" he attempts to ask.

Oh yeah, he doesn't know the Dark Spirit. He himself has never seen It. Like Vizor, Melok doesn't remember any event that occurred while the Unbound Evil controlled him.

"Melok, this is the Dark Spirit."

He finds it hard to believe that an embodiment of dark power could even exist because he lives in the "real" world. However, he then starts to think that this and the Chaos Prophecy are somewhat related.

"Does this...spirit have anything to do with that floating rock that you guys call a prophecy?"

"Well," the Dark Spirit says in Its spirit-like form, "yes and no."

"How's that?" Melok asks.

"The Solar Prophecies and I are not akin, but we have known each other for some time."

"So you guys have nothing to do with each other?" Melok tries to clarify.

"If you're talking about how they got here, then no."

"Okay, good," Melok is placing the puzzle pieces together in his mind. "Okay, this makes more sense. Anyway, can You open the box, Dark Spirit?"

"Well, Dark V..." I correct him since the Dark Spirit and I are technically one spirit now. "Yes, I can. Stand aside."

Melok scrambles away from the sarcophagus, but before I open it, I peek over to where Griff and Rodger have been fighting for a while now to see if they are okay. Both are hanging on by a thread. They need help, and quick. "Melok!"

Melok looks up in surprise. "Is something wrong?"

"Yes! Look!" I point to where Griff and Rodger are struggling.

Melok's eyes widen.

"I've got it, V, don't worry!" He rushes to the aid of my friends. I hope he makes it in time.

I place both of my hands on top of the golden lid of the sarcophagus. "Time to crack this walnut open." A dark blast awakens from my hands and shakes the sarcophagus so much that everyone within a mile radius trembles. The golden chamber cracks open just like I plan. A little too easily. I smell a rat - a divine, dark, and evil rat.

CHAPTER 22

The Alexandrian Police Force

s that really all I had to do? Did I really just have to use the Dark Spirit to open that tomb? This has "trap" written all over it. Where's the Unbound Evil? When I get my hands on It...Hold on...Calm down. The evil probably wants you like this to interrupt your thinking process. It wants me to focus more on It so I can't get to the Cave of Destiny. It wants the... Wait. It already has the prophecies' powers. This whole thing is a diversion! It really is using the prophecies' powers to create something that'll destroy the galaxy! I've got to warn everyone!

But still, the Chaos Prophecy is in the sarcophagus.

"Chaos Prophecy!" I look at it.

"Whoa!" The Chaos Prophecy is startled.

"Stand back, Vizor!"

"Wait!" It attempts to attack me. "It's me, V!"

"V?" The Chaos Prophecy thinks I'm a fake. But then the Dark Spirit makes Its spirit visible and says, "And Me. We can merge our spiritual makeups to make this embodiment of darkness, Dark V."

"You're using darkness to do this...?" The Chaos Prophecy floats in awe. "A hero usually uses the power of light."

"Should it matter?" I say. "They're both strong power sources with their own special abilities. Why not both? Isn't that what you're all about? Merging two opposites to create one all-powerful force?"

"I guess so." The Chaos Prophecy thinks about it.

"Rgh...!" The Chaos Prophecy lets go of something from its body that is purple and misty. The Unbound Evil, or at least a fragment of It.

The fragment of the Unbound Evil is so weak that it gets blown away instantly. That just proves the Unbound Evil is a parasite. It feeds off other's negative emotions, and uses them to Its advantage.

I look behind me. There are thousands of people on the floor, some badly injured, and some just tired from being possessed. Wait... Griff, Rodger, and Melok!

"Where are they?"

"Who?" The Chaos Prophecy is still regaining its balance after letting go the evil from inside.

"Griff, Rodger and Melok. I can't find them anywhere!"

"Huh, they're still here?" the Chaos Prophecy says. "All right, let's find them."

"Easier said than done," I say as I return to my normal state from Dark V. "Look around."

The Chaos Prophecy spins itself around to witness the casualties.

"The evil can possess this many people with a mere fragment of Its mind?" the prophecy muses aloud in fear.

I finally spot my friends. "There!" I run toward them, with the Chaos Prophecy floating behind me.

"Griff, Rodger, Melok!"

They're almost unconscious.

"Are you guys all right?"

It takes a few seconds, but I get a response.

"V–?" Melok stumbles to his feet. "Did you get the thing you were looking for?"

"See for yourself," the prophecy answers.

Melok looks toward the voice and peers closely to make sure the figure he's looking at is the Chaos Prophecy. Once he's satisfied, he dusts off his shirt.

"So what happened?" I ask Melok.

"I guess there were just too many of them to deal with."

"That many, huh?" I try to fathom the number of people. Then, a long silence occurs as if we are looking at a civil war amongst people that didn't have to fight in the first place. It is the Unbound Evil's fault. Why is It doing this? How badly has the Devil treated It all these years that It seems even more evil than the Devil Itself?

When the Earth was first created, the Unbound Evil killed my ancestors because of a disagreement, and now... It's all making sense now. Nothing has changed since the beginning of time. When there's a disagreement, one tries to eliminate the other and justifies it by classifying it as 'other'. It really is mind blowing that It never learns, and people are influenced by, and mimic, that same insane reasoning. Eliminating all you disagree with is never the answer. Destroying an entire world is not the answer.

There are many characters we've encountered that do not have to act as they do. Vizor acts like he doesn't like us at all, but in reality he has a very young mind. From the information we've gathered, the Unbound Evil has been controlling his thoughts and decisions for more than half his life. He hasn't lived yet. However, now, I daresay, the Unbound Evil is going to extremes to free Itself from the clutches of the Devil and create Its own identity and world. How exactly? It seems to be trying to function independent of the Devil and outdo It. Could this entire adventure, past and present, have been avoided if the Unbound Evil had understood that It shouldn't go to extremes no matter what? Has It not learned that there are at least two solutions to any problem, and eliminating an entire world is never a viable option? Suddenly, my thoughts are disrupted.

"V!" The Chaos Prophecy nudges my shoulder. "Look. Griff and Rodger are waking up!"

I see Griff starting to mumble, groan, and slowly lift his right arm.

"Griff! Rodger! Are you two okay? Oh no..." I inspect Rodger's right arm. As he tries to push up with it, he suddenly falls again. His arm is broken. Griff is in bad shape, too. His arm might be okay, but definitely not his leg. That is also broken.

"Your injuries got–" I start to say but Rodger finishes my thought. "I know...worse. Ow!"

A whirl of propellers sound from above. Finally, a sign of civilization. It feels like years since I've been around actual people, excluding Melok. They must've heard about the fighting because those helicopters are both police and emergency helicopters. I decide to wait because I want see if the "real" world will believe my story. If they don't, our whole adventure might end here. The helicopters land on the battlefield. Immediately, the officers rush over to us, I'm guessing because we're the only ones left standing. The policemen around us are armed, and for unknown reasons, the interrogation crew speaks English.

"Who are you, and what are you doing here?" an angry policeman asks.

"I'm V of San Francisco. It was a real nice place, if only it were still there. And where are you from?"

"Alexandria."

"Why weren't you here when the entire city was depopulated?"

"It wasn't."

"That's just not true. They came from King Tut's tomb over there, see?" I point over to the chamber that is still open.

"Baloney. All right, 'V of San Francisco', what are you doing on a war field?"

How did Alexandria not know of the entire population of Cairo disappearing? Is the Unbound Evil this good at what It does? Maybe It did step up Its game.

"Well actually..." I remember San Fran was wiped off the face of the map because of Zapzoid's remains. "San Francisco is gone too."

"Funny," the policeman says in a sarcastic tone. "Next you'll be tellin' me you saw King Tut. Ha! Give me a break."

Oh, he fails to see the irony there. Melok, standing next to me, sees the policeman's actions, and wants to help. He assumes if an adult confirms my story it will be more believable.

"He's not joking," Melok says in a sharp tone.

"Oh, yeah?"

The rifles start to point in Melok's direction.

"And who are you?"

Melok takes out some type of badge from his formal jacket. The policeman starts to shudder.

"I am Melok, member of the Federal Bureau of Investigation of the Unites States, originally from San Jose."

"WHAT?" I'm really surprised. "How come you never told us that?"

"Come now, V," Melok starts to explain, "do you really think I can tell everyone I meet I'm a member of the FBI? I had to make sure I could trust you first. I know I can now. I've got your back."

I give him a "V" sign. "Thanks, Melok." He understands the "V" symbol, nods, and turns toward the police officer who is impressed by Melok's position of authority.

"But if you are FBI," the policeman asks, "then why are you in Egypt?"

"My curiosity got the best of me," Melok explains. "They said they were going to Egypt because of a matter with King Tut, and that intrigued me, especially because these events could be linked to the destruction of San Francisco. I had, and still have, a curious mind that wanted more knowledge about a legend that we hardly know anything about."

"But you have duties, man!" The officer points at him. "You can't just abandon them."

"Oh, did I?" Melok raises an eyebrow. The policeman seems just as puzzled as I am.

"Melok, what do you mean you didn't leave your post as FBI?"

"You mean you haven't noticed yet, V? Where do you think Electrox is?"

Then it dawned on me that Electrox is supposed to be here next to us, but isn't. "How did it...? When did it...?"

"We talked it over," Melok stops my stuttering. "Electrox sensed that the big boom that we witnessed just meant more trouble for it, and we decided that it would go back and temporarily fill my post."

Now since that matter is settled, all we have to explain is how a few thousand people are lying unconscious on the ground.

"Even if you are part of the FBI," the policeman went on, "why are you on this war field?"

"First, I'll explain how this brawl began..."

Melok goes on and on for what seems like an eternity. He explains the spirit of King Tut, the Chaos Prophecy, Vizor, the Unbound Evil, and how the entire city of Cairo was trapped under the ground the best he can. Of course, we get the reaction I fear from the policeman.

"Do you honestly expect me to believe that the entire city of Cairo was trapped underground; that magical floating and talking rocks are one of the most powerful energy sources in the entire universe; that the Devil's disciple is terrorizing the Milky Way Galaxy; that King Tut's spirit is a thing; and that there are aliens with twin blades in their hair? You've got another think coming! Take them! Arrest them!"

Rodger steps in front of us in the nick of time. He authoritatively signals the policemen to stop. If Griff had done that, he would probably have gotten trampled, but given that Rodger is an adult and an authority figure, the policemen stop. Still, they are frustrated.

"Now what?" the same policeman yells. "What are you doing? Get behind me. You have orders!"

"No," Rodger says, "I don't."

"Another criminal."

The policeman judges again. People are so inconsiderate these days. How can you assume that a police officer, your own kind, wouldn't want all of these people saved? I've had enough.

–Dark Spirit! Show these people that spirits actually exist!

The area around me immediately becomes enveloped in a purple mist, and all of the surrounding policemen, even Rodger - I hope he's all right - are pushed back. My eyes start to radiate a purple mist, not like Dark V, but still a symbol that the Dark Spirit is within me. It's about time the world knew about the spirits. People can think what they want to, but I'm showing them the real truth.

"Ya believe me now?" I glare at the policemen.

"Monster...MONSTER! You're not human."

"He is obviously human, and obviously spirits do exist. Stop denying everything you see," Melok says in a tone that almost sounds like he's ordering the policeman. "Did it ever cross your mind to believe what we've just told you? If you know anything about this world, it's that anything is possible."

"I..." The policeman starts to get up. I can feel the policemen around me moving by the vibrations in the ground. All I'm doing now is making them see that my ideas are just as valid as theirs. We're all one unit, and this unit is called humanity.

The policemen jump at me with Tonfas and electric Tasers in clenched fists. With one backhand slap, all of them go flying a good ten feet.

"Call for backup!" the policeman cries.

"No!" I cry. "I don't want to hurt you. But the more you try to hurt me, the more I'll defend my friends and myself. You're blinded by fear and anger. Snap out of it!"

–V, the Dark Spirit calls from inside, *you know he'll keep assaulting all of you at this point. Why don't you brainwash him?*

–*Come on!* I'm disappointed at the Dark Spirit for even thinking I would do that. *As much as I want to get out of this mess, I want to teach this officer a lesson even more. Sorry, brainwashing just isn't my style. I don't slip my way out of situations like the Unbound Evil.*

–*I'm just concerned about you is all,* the Dark Spirit says in a friendly tone. *This passion you have for teaching humans the true values of life could lead to your demise.*

–*But my ultimate goal is to change the world for the better, Dark Spirit. I want people to see how awesome the world really is, no matter what the cost. That's why I'll keep fighting!*

–*Be careful is all I'm saying. I love your innate instinct for helping others. Just choose your battles wisely, all right?*

–*Thanks for the genuine concern.* I appreciate Its kind gesture.

The reinforcements are coming in from the sky and from the ground. A few tanks, helicopters, and fighter jets arrive. Thanks for the lemons guys, now let me make some lemonade for everyone.

The only problem is there are way too many pieces of weaponry. This could be tricky, especially since I don't want to hurt anyone. What should I do?

I hear more propeller and engine noises, only this time, they are coming from behind me. Oh no, it's the San Jose Police Department. I don't want people getting hurt. It's time I take a stand without fighting.

—I don't like this.

—Why not? the Dark Spirit asks. *Is it because you don't want them to fight?*

—Yeah. Why fight when you don't have to?

—Exactly, V. Fighting never solves anything. Actually, it could potentially create even more conflict.

—That's right. Let's go. I boost into the sky directly between the two opposing police forces.

"Alien!" the Alexandrian side shouts. I'm assuming the San Jose side believes in the Dark Spirit because they encountered tiny magnet people with a giant floating magnet as their king. Based on what they've already seen, I think they can believe anything is possible at this point.

"STOP!" I shout so loud that it echoes through the battlefield. Both forces stop in their tracks. San Jose's side seems relieved but Alexandria's side looks in fear. I think they would fire at any slip I make.

A policeman from the San Jose side shouts: "Get out of there, kid! Can't you see we're trying to help you?"

"On the contrary, you are making things worse."

"How?" the policeman shouts in frustration. "We're trying to make them see you're telling the truth!"

"By fighting." I exchange glances with both sides. "It never solves anything. It should only be a last resort. The Alexandrian police force at least asked what I was doing here. That was enough to show that they cared about the people here as much as I do."

"Why would you care about them?" someone asks from the Alexandrian side. "You're from San Francisco."

Again, English? How many Egyptians know English? That's something to think about later. Anyway, that comment made me furious.

"Don't judge a person by where they're from!" I shout back. "You're all policemen! Your job is to put aside differences for the greater good of everyone around you, not one small subgroup of people. That's not showing care and love for what you do."

The policemen start to talk amongst themselves, but I can't understand them because of all of the chatter.

"Kid, you're in the way of security actions. We can arrest–"

"Don't even start with that." My tone changes to the Dark V tone. Immediately, the Alexandrian side opens fire. Every missile, bullet, and grenade they shoot at me goes straight through me.

The Alexandrian commander, who turns out to be the policeman who interrogated me, shouts, "Oh no, nothing's working. All personnel, cease fire! Retreat!"

As they try to escape, I fly to the other side and block their exit.

They're trapped.

"Please, have mercy," the Alexandrian commander begs.

This is my chance. "Didn't you hear me before?" I shout back. "I don't want to hurt you. Commander. Give me a chance, listen to me."

This time, the commander tells his men to hold their fire and smiles.

"First, prove you're human and reveal the 'spirit' within you. Then I'll give you a chance."

"Certainly." The Dark Spirit's chemical makeup starts to lift from my spirit. The two of us separate. To make sure the commander and his crew believe us, the Dark Spirit comes into physical view. The Alexandrian police force should see It now.

Little did I know this would be a serious mistake.

"Hello everyone. I am the divine Dark Spirit. I am pleased to meet your acquaintance."

At sight of this, the commander and his entire team gasp in awe.

As soon as the commander realizes the Dark Spirit is real, he screams, "NOW!"

A tube falls from a helicopter overhead. It is going for the Dark Spirit. Don't they realize by now that you can't trap a spirit? It doesn't matter because the Dark Spirit dodges the tube. Someone needs to tell all of these guys not everything in life that is different from you is meant to be tortured. It could be as simple as listening, really listening. Apparently, the Alexandrian police force doesn't believe in anything that "little runts" tell them. Now, I think it's safe to say I can show them who the real runts are, and guess what? I'm not going to lay a finger on anyone to do so. I am more than capable of showing them my real power without hurting them physically. I can't say the exact same thing for them and their mental state.

"Guys," I start, "really? After I trusted you?"

"You honestly think we're going to change our ways because of a kid?"

"Actually, I was hoping you would. Age really doesn't matter. I mean, I've been one step ahead of you this entire time. You couldn't sneak up on me to save your lives. I've outsmarted you and I'm definitely more morally sound. Face actual reality for once in your life."

"I can easily have you ruined you know." The commander is furious over the fact that I'm correct and he's, well…not.

"Oh, that's funny. For what? What crime have I committed that is worth arresting me over?"

"For interfering with national security. That's what!"

"That's another funny one. Sounds like to me, and the rest of your crew, that you're the ones committing the crimes here."

"Rules are different here, kid," the commander says. "I can have you hung by the gallows. This is Egypt, not San Francisco."

"In what place on this green Earth can you strap innocent people to a rope and call that okay?"

"The place I run! You don't tell me what to do! Got that? I am the judge of you! I am your superior! Respect me!"

"Don't have to." I cross my arms as a sign of disrespect. "You give me no reason to respect you, and because of that, I'll crush you. It'll be a cakewalk."

"Go ahead and try! Ready men? FIRE!"

–Dark Spirit!

–Right!

It knows immediately what to do. We merge just in time. The bullets go through me again.

–I was thinking we should trap them in a shield. What do You say?

–Great idea! The Dark Spirit sounds pleased. *I love how you don't*

want to hurt them, even after they've tried to capture Me.

—I just want them to recognize their own stubbornness, and to hear and consider my ideas. After explaining my reasoning to the Dark Spirit, I snap my fingers.

"What are you doing?" The commander starts clenching his left fist.

"Oh nothing," I respond. "Come at me. I dare you!"

That sets him off. My plan works. See how easily people can be blinded by hate and anger?

The commander dashes toward me, but he hits something really hard and falls on his back. He ran into an invisible barrier that the Dark Spirit put up at my command.

"What is this?" the commander asks.

"A wall. A barrier to make sure you and your little *gang* don't go anywhere."

"Did you just call my squad...?"

"Well, you're not a police force. All you've been doing is trying to bully me. You haven't given me a solid chance, while I've given you several. Again, I don't want to harm you. Just give me a chance, please."

"If you were our ally, you'd let us do our jobs and you would admit that you committed a crime."

"What crime? What could I have possibly done wrong?"

"You got in the way of national security..."

"For the bajillionth time, I am innocent and have no reason to interfere with your security!"

"Except you're not innocent," the commander says. "You're a suspect, and you gave us a fairy tale when we asked what happened here. You think we can actually trust you?"

"But my story really did happen. How many times do I have to tell you?"

"You tell me..." The commander's tone suddenly changed to a happier one.

—V! Behind you!

I look around and find another Alexandrian police officer trying to ambush me. I've lost all respect for the commander now. I'll show no mercy.

"You disgust me. I could just let you sit there and die, but that would be cowardly on MY part." I snap my fingers again and the invisible barrier vanishes. Immediately, the commander yells, "FIRE! Make sure nothing remains of his corpse!"

Not surprisingly, they forget that every shot they shoot passes through me.

"Idiots."

I prepare to fly past all of the police line at the speed of sound to cause a little mayhem. However, as I am about to launch, something lands around me. It's a giant tube. Really? I can just walk through it like so... Uh-oh. Gas! It's too late. I breathe it in and I can't move. I'm paralyzed.

–No...!

"Haha!" the commander shouts. "Got 'em! Hold your fire, men."

"V!" Melok yells from a distance. He rushes over, or at least he tries. The police squad that kept him busy while I was scuffling with the commander stops him from going any further.

–Dark Spirit.

–What is it, V?

–Help Melok get me out of this jam.

–Got it! I'll try my best! The Dark Spirit escapes from the tube and proceeds toward Melok.

"Out of my way!" Melok says as the Dark Spirit enters him. Melok starts to shudder because he doesn't know what is going on within his body.

–What...? Melok thinks.

–It's okay, Melok. The Dark Spirit tries to calm him down.

–Who are you?

–The legendary Dark Spirit.

–THE Dark Spirit? Melok is amazed. *So You can do anything I ask You to do?* He smirks.

–Well, within reason. V trusts that you will use proper human judg-ment.

—All right, then here's what I'm thinking... Melok starts to, in his mind, come up with a plan to save me, prove my innocence, and help the Alexandrian police force realize that spirits exist. How on Earth is he going to do all of that? Maybe he isn't...I'm not sure.

"Why are you smiling?" the policeman asks him.

"Do you really want to know?" he says in the voice of the Dark Spirit. He then exerts a purple mist from his body and reveals that his eyes are purple.

"How...?"

"Don't just stand there, men!" the commander shouts. "Fire!"

"Don't you learn?" Melok says - still in the Dark Spirit's voice. He proceeds to walk past everyone as if they were specs of dust in the wind. The men can't shoot nor grab Melok because the Dark Spirit is helping him. He barges through everyone and goes straight to the commander.

"Please don't hurt me," he begs for mercy.

"You treat people unfairly," Melok says in his own voice, "so expect the same treatment. I'm placing you under arrest!"

"Oh, really?" The stubborn commander just doesn't quit.

Oh well, I think Melok will make him quit.

"Ugh..."

I look over and see that the commander's collar is in Melok's hand.

"Where's the key to the tube?" Melok asks.

"There is none..."

"LIES!" Melok throws him to the ground.

"How...? Why can't I touch you?" the commander asks.

"The power of spirits are real, commander, and it's not something that humans can just take to a test tube and study. We don't like it when you forcefully take things in the name of 'science' and 'human evolution'. I'm starting to think you weren't even going to study the Dark Spirit. Maybe you were just going to drain the life out of It and harness Its energy to secretly construct something very destructive. It's not hard to see that you're a power hungry coward. Commander, you're through. Just give up with whatever pride you have left."

"How?" the commander says in frustration. "It's that kid, isn't it? He's the mastermind behind all of this."

"Think what you want, commander, but it won't matter. No one will even listen to you anymore because you're not trustworthy. Look at your own police force." The commander turns and finds the two sides have merged together.

"They're one unit now, and they're on our side. We've won. Thanks, Melok."

CHAPTER 23

The Ultimate Reunion

Whew! Thanks for the hand Melok. "Hey!" I scream, banging on the tube. As the commander is being carried away, Melok notices my banging noises and remembers that I am still trapped inside this test tube. He asks the Alexandrian policeman how to unlock the tube.

"All you have to do is unscrew the huge cap on the top."

"With my bare hands?"

"It's a lot lighter than you think." The guard smiles.

Melok undoes the top of the tube like it's the cap of a water bottle. It really is that easy, huh?

I jump out of the tube. "Thanks a bunch, Melok!" I give him a "V" sign.

"It's nothing. We're friends, remember?"

He really does value our friendship. That means a lot to me. Oh yeah, speaking of friends, "Hey, may I have the Dark Spirit back now?"

"Yeah, sure you can."

–What do I do? Melok asks the Dark Spirit.

–What are you talking about? the Dark Spirit asks.

–You know, how do I properly transfer You back to V?

–There's no proper way, really, but thanks for your concern. The Dark Spirit lifts from Melok's body and places Itself back into my body.

–You there? I think to myself.

–As I should be.

–Good.

It's time I finally went back to the Cave of Destiny. After all, it is where that huge tablet told me to go. And considering that the tablet was inside the official Solar Prophecies' temple, I believe it is the right thing to do. However, first I have to make sure that Griff and Rodger are okay.

"Where did Griff and Rodger go? Are they okay?"

"Both of them went to one of Cairo's hospitals," Melok replies. "While you were busy with the commander, I had my men take them to a nearby hospital because they were both badly injured. After that, the Alexandrian Police Force kept me busy."

"Then let's go pay them a visit. I can heal them with the power of the Dark Spirit, like I did before."

"Before?" Melok looks puzzled.

"Right before we met."

"Ah, okay."

We head toward Cairo, and let the San Jose Police Department handle everything in the battlefield. As we head toward the hospital, I stop for a moment, turn around, and shout to all the policemen, "Thanks you guys! You were a huge help." I give them all a "V" sign.

We make it to the hospital, and sure enough, the only people we find there are Griff, Rodger, and two medics from the San Jose Police Department. They don't look too happy.

"How are they?" I ask.

"They're in critical condition. You can't be in here!" one says.

"Actually, I can help them wake up."

"But that'll take days to..." the other one starts.

"Trust him," Melok says. "Let him through."

"If you say so, sir," they say in unison.

I go up to Griff and Rodger and place my hands on their chests. I take a deep breath. A dark mist exits my hands and disappears into both of them. The doctors gasp at this, and they nearly faint as Griff and Rodger grumble and try to sit up. Finally, they regain full consciousness.

"Wha...V?" Griff holds his head in pain. "Is that you? Where are we?"

"Yeah, Griff, it's me."

"Did you use the Dark Spirit again?"

"How could I not? I know you guys would rather help me save the galaxy than sit here in this hospital."

"You know us too well," Rodger says moaning a bit.

"But it's your call, guys. I don't want to make you guys do something you don't want to. It all depends on how you feel. How do you–?"

Griff cuts in. "Are you kidding? There's no way we'll miss this. I've already missed a lot, and I want to make up for lost time. I'm ready when you are, V!"

"The same applies for me, V," Rodger cuts in. "I'm still here with you. 100% of the way."

"I knew I could always count on you guys. Come on, I know where we're going next. The Cave of Destiny."

Griff's eyes widen. "We're going back there?"

–*Wait, V, the Dark Spirit stops me. How do you know we have to go to the Cave of Destiny?*

–*You must not have been with me when I saw it. That or You were just snoozing inside of me. We have to go to the Cave of Destiny because the pharaoh showed me the master tablet with the picture of Your phoenix on it.*

–*Did it just show that?*

–*Yeah. Why?*

–*Oh no. I don't think we have to go to the Cave of Destiny.*

–*Why's that? Didn't I find You there?*

–*Yes, but where was My picture originally located? There was a picture of a castle, not of Me, in the Cave of Destiny.*

–*Oh dear God, Vizor's castle...*

–*I'm afraid so, but why? Why would the tablet want you there? Could something be waiting for us there?*

–*Only one way to find out.*

"Hey, guys? I think I realize where we REALLY have to go now..." I say nervously. "Vizor's castle."

"WHAT?" Griff and Rodger bellow. They don't seem too happy.

"How could you come to that conclusion, V?" Melok asks.

"King Tut showed me a big tablet in the prophecies' main chamber. It showed me the picture of the Dark Spirit that was in Vizor's castle. At first, I thought it meant to go to the place I originally met the Dark Spirit. But now I think it means that we have to go where that picture was originally located. Even if that's not our final destination, we're probably going to find something in Vizor's Castle."

"I guess," Griff says. "But I don't like the sound of this. What if it's another trap?"

"If it is another trap," Melok says, "we'll face it together."

"But is there another way?" Rodger asks.

"We could split up," Melok brainstorms, "but that'll just make it harder to find us if something happens. Actually, I think we should all go together. It might be slower, but we could face any trap the Unbound Evil has placed for us that way."

"Melok's right," I say. "Let's go together guys. Time's a waistin'!"

We exit the hospital, and think about the power of flight.

As we ascend a few feet, I ask, "We all good, guys?" They all give me a thumbs up. "Then let's go!"

We fly to the outer limits of the solar system. All of us slowly descend to the ground. Griff, Rodger, and I inspect Vizor's Castle to see if anything has changed. From the looks of it, nothing has. Just to make sure, I check with the Dark Spirit and the Chaos Prophecy.

–Anything, Dark Spirit?

–Yes. The Unbound Evil is ahead, as well as the Devil. They're probably expecting you.

–I could verify that, says the Chaos Prophecy. *Both the Devil and the Unbound Evil are definitely in there.*

"So this is Vizor's castle..." Melok gazes in wonder. "Intriguing. Guys, anything I should know before we go in?"

"Just beware of the many traps scattered throughout," Griff warns, "and you should be just fine!"

I remember the concern I had earlier. If the Unbound Evil wants the prophecies' energy to destroy my galaxy and build Its own empire, why is the Devil here? And why doesn't It just take my prophecy from me? Is It just luring me into a trap so It doesn't have to come find me?

What a lazy coward. I guess I should expect nothing less from It. After all, It is the prince of all things negative. More importantly, if It has four of the five prophecies, It just needs mine to complete Its quest. I need a plan.

As everyone starts toward the castle, I stop. "Guys, wait."

Everyone pauses and looks back.

"The Unbound Evil only needs the Chaos Prophecy, right? So why is the Devil here? And more importantly, why am I about to walk in with the Chaos Prophecy knowing that..."

"Because I have these six with Me," an all too familiar voice bellows. Immediately, Griff, Rodger, and I recognize the voice and what It's talking about. The Unbound Evil is here, and It has our families!

A dark spiral materializes in front of us. As soon as it subsides, the Unbound Evil appears.

"What's up, rodents?" It smiles maniacally.

"You have them with you right now? GIVE THEM BACK!" I say in an angry tone.

Melok turns in confusion and fear because he has never heard me use such an angry tone. "Calm down V. What does It have?"

Rodger answers for me. "The Unbound Evil has had their families for years. That's why I'm their legal guardian."

"You?" Melok says in a shocked voice. "You're their legal guardian, and you let them come on this dangerous journey? Are you nuts?"

"It was a hunt for their families. I had no idea such forces were involved. But if it's for the sake of the galaxy, how could I hold these two potential heroes back?"

Melok stares with awe and disgust.

−Does he have that much faith in these two? How could Rodger put these innocent kids in harms way when he could just call authorities and have them do it for them?

−Hmm... The Unbound Evil starts to realize the frustration inside of Melok's head. *I could use him again, and this time, the pharaoh is with me.* The Unbound Evil flies toward Melok, and enters his body.

"Ugh...!" Melok falls to his knees. "Get out of my head. You monster!"

"No can do, Melok! I will stay in here as long as I please, got it? I don't care how you feel. I just need those three out of my sight. Now cooperate!"

"Melok!" I get his attention. "The evil feeds off negative emotions. What could you possibly be feeling now that's negative?"

Melok's eyes widen in surprise. He explains himself. "Why would Rodger ever let you two go on this journey? I just want you two out of harm's way. It's what I've always wanted to do, protect people."

"We understand, Melok," Griff cuts in, "but a part of being friends and family is the ability to trust and support each other. If we can't trust each other to carry out specific tasks, then we can't have faith in each other. If we can't trust each other, then we can't have a pure bond. I know it seems impossible for anyone so young to do this, but we've done pretty well so far. During this crazy journey, we've actually had the adventure of a lifetime."

"Adventure of a lifetime?" the Unbound Evil repeats. "How can this ordeal be the adventure of a lifetime?"

"It depends on how you look at it," Griff answers. "The only reason this adventure has been dangerous is because of You. You've gotten in our way too many times. On the flip side, V, Rodger, and I have strengthened our bond as a family tenfold. No other experience could have done that. So thanks for that, but now it's time we put You to sleep, forever!"

"Insolent little..." the Unbound Evil starts.

"Don't even start. All of Your threats have been in vain so far, Unbound Evil. Look at You; You're actually afraid of us!"

"I don't care what you think of Me! All I need is My plan. If you're going to act all high and mighty and think you're above Me, then I'll be happy to cause you even more despair than you've already felt!"

"What do You mean?"

"Come on out, My slaves!"

Out of the ground come the people that we've been trying to find for what seems like eternity, Griff's and my families.

"Guys!" I reach for them, but then realize they can't hear me. Something's not right. I feel their presence but they aren't entirely here. I have to muster all my strength to remain focused and not be overwhelmed and blinded by emotion. "What have You done to them?"

"I've merely shown them what kind of person you are." Melok is still struggling.

"What are you talking about?"

"You're trying to stop Me from creating a utopia! Why would you sacrifice your families to do that? What would your family think of you? Why don't you ask them, V?"

"How about I ask You to set them free before You get what's coming to You?"

"I'd be delighted to, but I have better things to attend to, like the prophecies!"

Uh-oh. I look around and the Chaos Prophecy is nowhere to be found.

"Next time think twice before trying to get too comfortable with Me! DON'T EVER SAY OR EVEN THINK I'M NOT TO BE RECKONED WITH! But now, it doesn't even matter. You can't stop your galaxy from being destroyed! In the meantime, I'll keep you here with your family. After all, you guys need to...CATCH UP! HAHAHAHAHAHAHA! See you guys later! I've got a utopia to create...AND DESTROY!" The Unbound Evil, in Melok's body, jumps back inside of the castle. Vizor's castle slowly elevates. After it reaches its destined height, it dashes toward the center of the galaxy. In the process, all of us (including my family) are flung down to the icy grounds of Pluto.

"Hello, V," my little bro, D, says. "So glad to see you...give me a hug!" He tries to grab at me, but if you look closely, he's obviously trying to hurt me. How can I snap them out of their current state without harming them? Is there a way? Do I really have to fight my own family?

"Griff?" I see he's in a ditch.

"Yeah?"

"Help me! Your family and my family are trying to kill me!"

"Stand back, V," Rodger says. "Let me do this."

"No, I want to..."

"No you don't, I know you. This would hurt you more than it would hurt them. Sit this one out, all right? Griff, follow V!"

"Fine, but please don't harm them! Go for their heads." Out of context, that just sounds evil.

"I'll do what I can." Rodger smiles. "Take cover, just in case something happens."

I nod and head for the nearest boulder. Griff eventually slides out of the crevice he is in and comes toward me. Rodger prepares for combat. As they are about to make contact with each other, a yellow orb of light darts down at an incredibly high speed. Its impact is so great that it sends everyone, except Griff and me, a good ten feet back.

–*Hey!* The Dark Spirit realizes, but hardly believes, what it is.

"V!" The orb dashes toward me. "I escaped the Unbound Evil's grasp!"

"I see. Nice! How do you feel?"

"Good as new!" King Tut answers. "What's going on? Who are those possessed people?"

"That's Griff's and my family."

"What?" The pharaoh is stunned. "It got to them too?"

"Actually, they were taken from me when I was seven years old. I haven't seen them for six years, and this is not the reunion I had imagined. I haven't the slightest clue how to fight my own family to rip the Unbound Evil out of their heads."

"Oh..." The pharaoh takes all of that in, and then gets an idea. "Wait! You don't have to fight them! I can erase the evil out of their minds with ancient Egyptian magic."

"Please!" I beg him. "Please save them! I can't wait to give them all a big, huge hug!" I am overwhelmed with emotion. I've missed them all so much. Just seeing them again blows my mind. I am stunned, almost paralyzed. I thought, for sure, the Unbound Evil was going to kill them.

"Watch closely." The pharaoh charges toward Z, my older brother, but is easily deflected by Z's hand. King Tut flies back and lands in my arms. "Ow! How did that happen?"

–It must be the Unbound Evil, V! Its power is canceling out the pharaoh's! He's not able to enter their bodies.

"I know!" I grab the pharaoh's spirit with my right hand. It erupts into a radiant yellow orb.

"V...?" The pharaoh is confused.

"Hey, Rodger!" I throw the ball of light at him.

"What am I supposed to do with this?" Rodger asks.

"You have to manually place the pharaoh's spirit in the back of each of their heads. That way, the pharaoh can work its magic on all of them. It might take a little while, but this just might work!"

Rodger nods, then turns around to find our families stumbling up. There are six: my mom and dad, D, Z, and Griff's mom and dad. Rodger wastes no time and instantly darts toward D. He jumps over D and lightly taps the back of his head. D faints, falls down, and the Unbound Evil is lifted from his body. Rodger then does it again to Z, Griff's parents, then my mom and dad, and eventually cures everyone of the plague that is the Unbound Evil. Rodger takes a knee from exhaustion.

"Are they all right?" Griff extends his hand out toward his mom and dad. His eyes start to water. Then, D starts to grumble. I run toward him. Griff follows behind me, and races toward his parents.

"D!" I start to cry. His eyes open. I haven't seen him since he was a tiny toddler. He has slight curls in his dark brown hair, and his giant, brown eyes crown his beautifully lit face.

"Hi V!" His eyes water. I hug him tight. I am never letting the Unbound Evil touch these guys ever again. Shortly after, Z gets up, regaining complete strength and consciousness.

"V? Come here buddy!"

He runs, arms open, toward me. His appearance is a lot different from mine. He basically looks like an older version of D, except he has straight hair and a giant beard because he hasn't shaven in a while.

Our parents get up next.

"V?" My mom bursts into happy tears. Her mix of light brown hair looks like a chocolate wave headed toward me on a majestic, slightly wrinkled face with loving, brown eyes. "Oh, I'm so glad you're safe! You've grown so much!"

"V!" My dad follows. He is fairly tall, with buzzed down, gray hair. His face looks like an older version of mine. His beard has grown long as well. "Come here and brace yourself for the biggest hug you've ever gotten!"

"Guys!" I gasp for air. "You're crushing me..."

"Sorry." My dad says. "I missed you too much. We all missed you!" This is one big, happy family reunion. I picture us having a picnic, with my mom making all the food. That's something I really miss: mom's cooking (because between you and me, Rodger can't cook). Dad would take us all to a lush hill in his giant truck, and my two brothers would be sitting in the back with me. Good times...almost as good as these hugs.

Griff is reuniting with his parents also. "Mom! Dad!" He bursts into tears.

"Griff!" they cry. "It's so great to finally be back together," Griff's dad says.

"That...*Thing* was awful to us!" Griff's mom shudders. I overhear this, and realize that the only reason this is happening is because of the Unbound Evil. IT'S GOING TO PAY! I then remember that It, in Vizor's castle, is headed toward the sun, with the prophecies. Uh-oh. We've got to stop It!

"Guys! I don't have time to explain. We have to get to the sun. Now!"

"What? Are you on a suicide mission or just want a nice tan? Last I checked, the sun couldn't sustain life." Z definitely hasn't lost his sense of humor.

My dad places his hand on my mom's shoulder. They look away. They feel bad for not telling me, and for getting me into this heap of trouble.

"You guys knew all along, didn't you?"

"Sorry, V," my mom apologizes. "We didn't want to expose you to such negativity at such a young age. We couldn't live with ourselves. We knew you'd find out someday, but we never realized it'd be so soon."

Z and D are just plain lost now.

"Okay, what's going on?" D is scratching his head.

"We'll explain on our way to the sun, but basically, I'm supposed to save the world from a divine evil."

"Heh?" Z grunts. "Well, you weren't much different in school. Yeah, we know all about *that* day at that awful school. The Unbound Evil showed us as an attempt to make us lose hope. But to us, it was a sign that you were figuring out who you are. We were happy to see you knock down that bully."

I'm in shock. I didn't know my family knew about what I'd been through.

"Mom..." I approach her. "I know your maternal instincts want me safe, but you have to understand, I have to finish this. Do you have any idea what's at stake?"

"Yes." My mom's eyes water a little bit. "But we don't want you exposing yourself to such horrid forces. We can't afford to lose you. Never again..."

"Look, mom," I grab her shoulder and smile, "thanks for trying to protect me, but now I can take this. I'm strong on the inside, and I have been for a while."

"I guess you're not the little boy I tucked into bed just a few short years ago. It seems like an eternity, but at the same time, like yesterday. You're a teenager now who grew up too fast and has the life experiences of a young man. I trust your judgment. Do what you must. And we'll be here to support you."

"Let's just say things went downhill since you guys left. But they're getting better, and they'll continue to get better because you guys are here with me now." We all smile and look at each other.

Suddenly, it gets warmer, and we hear a violent shake in the distance. The sun! The Unbound Evil and the Devil must've gotten to it already. We have to get there, and fast!

"Uh-oh!" Griff says. "V, we've got to get going!"

"Guys," I say to my family, "we don't have time to drop you off at Earth. Come on, fly with us!" They all start to scan the surrounding area.

"Uhh..." Z is lost. "Where's your rocket?"

"We don't have one," Rodger says, having observed our reunion from the sidelines. King Tut is right next to him, steadily hovering near his shoulder. "We fly by our own will because our belief in ourselves is that powerful."

"We've learned a great deal about the world during this journey, guys," Griff says to everyone just rescued. "And one of those things is that the way to take control of your life is to believe that you have the strength to do anything you want. The Solar Prophecies taught us that."

"The Solar Prophecies?" D and Z look at each other equally flabbergasted.

"We'll explain later," I tell them. "Do you guys truly have our backs?" D, Z, Mom, and Dad all take a look at each other and nod one by one.

Z then looks me in the eyes and says, "All the way, V! And we know you have ours!"

"This is our adventure now, too!" D adds with the passion and eagerness of a 10-year-old.

I give them my famous "V" sign. "I knew I could count on my family to always be there for me. You guys are irreplaceable. Welcome back! Rise up, my friends and family!" I lift my arms up as a sign for them to try and fly. "You guys can do it! Believe in your own strength and focus on it! Nothing is impossible when you trust yourself and those around you. Let's go!"

CHAPTER 24

The Final Confrontation

It takes them a few minutes, but eventually they start to slightly elevate, and are thoroughly amazed by the thrill.

"Wow, cool!" D starts to do backflips in the air.

"Now this is massive air time!" Z jokes.

"Let's go, guys. Time to finally save our galaxy from the Unbound Evil's and the Devil's wrath!" We head toward the sun for our final battle.

On the way, I try to explain the best I can to Z and D what my legacy is and how it came to be. After I finish, D is a little frightened, and Z can hardly believe what just came out of my mouth.

"You can't be serious." Z is trying to digest all the information. "That's unbelievable!"

"I can't make you believe anything. What you believe is up to you. You wanted some answers, and I gave you what I know."

Z finally starts to fathom how the extraordinary story I told him can be true. "I guess anything's possible when the Devil shows up at your front door and utterly destroys everything around It."

"But how are we involved in this?" D starts to wonder. "We're brothers, right? Shouldn't we be a part of this?"

"Perhaps. But as of right now, I don't think you two are directly involved in my legacy. I mean, I might not even know the entire thing, so I can't really answer that question."

D is a little uncomfortable with that. "Then how can we help...?"

"By being there for him." My dad steps in. "True this age old legacy is his alone and is critically important, but all heroes draw strength and confidence from somewhere. We're the ones who are going to help him out the most. That makes us a big part of his legacy as well. We're always here for you, V, even if divine forces are in play. If anyone's vibrant spirit will find a way, it's yours. You are truly the man for the job." After one last group hug, Vizor's castle is in view. Brace yourselves, guys. This is probably going to be the biggest fireworks show you've ever seen.

The heat is getting worse by the minute, yet no one seems to be affected by it. It appears like everyone here catches on quickly. The happiness and completeness I feel with my family makes me feel stronger than ever. Good to know these guys really do have my back 'till the end. We'll need all the firepower we can muster. Together, it should be enough to take down any opposing force. The best way to test it for sure is to move forward. The Unbound Evil, the Devil, the sun, the Solar Prophecies, and Vizor's castle are dead ahead.

"I was expecting you all sooner," the Unbound Evil 'welcomes' us. "But as you might've feared, you're already too late. The prophecies have been gathered, and now all I have to do is drain them of their power."

"It's time for this galaxy to be gloriously reborn." The Devil smirks.

"Not as long as we're here!" Griff shouts. "You might have divine power, but you two can't fathom the strength we have. The bonds we share with each other give us power like You couldn't even begin to imagine!"

"That's because it's feeble and weak!" the Unbound Evil roars. "You let the prophecies get taken from right under your noses. Who needs friends like that? What kind of friends are you?"

"Ones who can feel each other's presence without them even being there," I add. "You've obviously, never had that."

"Like I care about what you pathetic humans have to say," the Devil announces proudly. "I have eyes and ears everywhere through my loyal servants. Especially the Unbound Evil. He was nice enough to rebuild this galaxy in Our–"

"MY image!" The Unbound Evil binds the Devil to four solar

flares. It can't escape.

"What? I thought we're in this together!"

"Please! YOU'RE THE REASON I'M DOING THIS, MASTER!"

The Devil is actually struggling. Did It really give the Unbound Evil equal power? Did the Devil actually trust something? I thought It was the King of Negativity and had no soul. Unbelievable. The King of Trickery just got tricked.

"AAARRRGGHHH!" the Devil cries in pain. "NOOO...WHAT ARE YOU DOING?!"

"WHAT I SHOULD'VE DONE EONS AGO, DESTROYING THIS UNIVERSE!"

"What?" King Tut says. "But You'll destroy Yourself in the process."

"No I won't! I am always a step ahead of the game. I'm going to use my Father as a shield! I'll place It in the bomb, and that'll be that! At least it won't harm Me."

"But You can't destroy the Devil! It's immortal." Z points out.

"Not in a world where I make the rules!"

"It isn't Your world." A mighty voice shakes the fabric of time so powerfully that it echoes through the emptiness of space.

"I should've known." The Unbound Evil smirks a bit. "Welcome to the show."

A giant orb of light appears out of thin air and illuminates everything within a hundred-mile radius.

"Your insane plans end here and now!" I proclaim. Ready everyone?" We all look at the Devil as if we are expecting It to help stop the Unbound Evil. But when we look around, the Devil disappears into Vizor's castle.

"Hey, come back!" Rodger throws his fist in the air. "I didn't even see It move an inch."

"What do you think It's going to do?" I ask.

Griff shrugs. "For all I know the Devil might want to destroy the galaxy *before* the Unbound Evil does. I mean, that's what I'd think It'd do." In mere seconds, we see what looks like a shooting star strike the

Unbound Evil.

"OWW!" It yelps in pain. "Who...?"

"Don't even bother asking!" No way –VIZOR? How did he know we're here? Wait...

–*Do you feel it?* I ask the Dark Spirit.

–*How can I not? This is the most incredible power Vizor has exerted so far, V.*

"No one out manipulates me!" Vizor shouts in the Devil's voice. "I should've known You were nothing but trouble, Unbound Evil. Prepare to die." The Devil and the Unbound Evil prepare themselves to battle in a fight to the death. But I see right through the Unbound Evil's plan.

I dash between the two of them with an attempt to keep them apart: "Stop! Devil, don't You get it? It's just manipulating You further. Your anger is blinding You! Get a grip!"

"Well," the Unbound Evil starts, "I can't have you exposing my plans any further. V, you're dead."

"Not as long as I'm here," Z steps up.

"And me," my mom steps up.

"V's not going anywhere!" my dad says.

"I'll help too!" D cutely swims forward.

"Aww, how precious. I'll finally kill all of you! This is adorable. The family will forever be together again!"

"Wait..." the Devil barely mouths. "I'll help you too. V..."

"Oh no, You won't!" The sun shoots out multiple solar flares and ensnares the Devil. "No!" The Devil is slowly being pulled toward the sun.

"You're going to be the final power source for My galactic bomb! HAHAHAHA!"

"You're not going to do anything on my watch, Unbound Evil!" I protest. "My bond with everyone here is stronger than Your bomb will ever be, and that's power You can't compete with. And this is the power I'll use to crush You. Your malicious plans end here!"

"I'd love to see You try," the evil responds.

"Well how's this for trying?" I close my eyes. Prophecies, answer me!

"Not this time!" The Unbound Evil shoots out Its absorbing tentacles. I try to dodge them, but find myself ensnared despite my efforts.

"V!" everyone shouts.

I keep my eyes closed, trying to tap into the prophecies' power.

–*Solar Prophecies!* I try to reach them. *Help me lay waste to the Unbound Evil's plans! Please!*

–*We can't escape, V,* the Wisdom Prophecy says. *Even if we did, it wouldn't do us any good. It'd be like taking the sun out of space. The solar system would freeze, and Earth would come to an end.*

On that note, I block out everything around me and listen to the voice in my head: This is it, V. This is the climax of this journey. Everything you've been through is now put to a final test. Everyone's here, and if we fail to stop the evil's plans now, we'll never be able to reverse the damage.

I have to believe in myself now more than ever. It's time I showed the true power of the prophecies.

"You're finished!" I shout. Incredible heat and light energy miraculously erupts around me and burns the tentacles, freeing me from the Unbound Evil's trap. "Enter EXTREME V!"

My transformation doesn't take long, mere seconds. My eyes glow, my hair goes crazy, and I give off incredible amounts of energy. Extreme V is back and better than ever.

"NO!" The Unbound Evil is confused. "Impossible, the prophecies' power is still in the sun!"

"That may be, but my power is still inside of me. Like I said, that's something You can never take away!"

"I don't care where your power comes from," the Unbound Evil says. "All I care about is anything that opposes the utopia I am about to create. This is your end. Prepare to be eliminated, all of you! My bomb will detonate any second now, and I need some entertainment to pass the time. You all will be My playthings, while I watch the galaxy being destroyed."

I have to get everyone out of here! If they stay, they'll be destroyed by the cosmic blast. Wait...

–*Dark Spirit...? You still feel Vizor, right?*

–Yes. I'm still trying to figure out how he's alive and well. Why is the energy I feel from him increasing? And more importantly, how is the bomb's energy decreasing? Is Vizor absorbing the prophecies AND the Devil? Is that even possible? Remember chaos? the Dark Spirit points out.

Of course! Combining the negative energy with the prophecies' positive energy...

Then I get another idea. What if all these guys were to have the extreme power I possess? The evil would be in for the biggest brawl this galaxy has ever seen. Let's do it! Wait, speaking of all of these guys, where's Melok?

"Griff! Rodger! Where's Melok?"

We were all so happy to be reunited again that we forgot about him! Where could he have gone? Then we all come to a silent conclusion.

"What'd you do with him this time?" Griff points in the Unbound Evil's direction. "This is getting old, even for You."

"What are you talking about?" The Unbound Evil looks confused.

"Don't play this game with us again. We all know You have him, so why don't You just hand him over before this gets ugly?"

"Oh you mean Melok," the Unbound Evil finally concludes after looking around. "Something had to be done about him. If I hadn't done what I did, My plan wouldn't go as..."

"What did you do to him?" Rodger is enraged.

"I'd be more concerned about yourselves because..." The Unbound Evil then realizes the bomb's energy is almost completely drained. "What? Where's the energy?"

Something inside the sun then begins to brighten.

"Oh, I'd duck right now," Z says.

Vizor then flies out of the sun and releases a lot of energy in the process. He looks different. His dark blue hair has caught fire, his red eyes have turned a deep crimson, and he now exerts a mysterious, dark force.

"Impossible!" the Unbound Evil says. "I thought You were drained."

"I guess what those humans say is true," the Devil in Vizor says. "What doesn't kill you makes you stronger. Although, since I'm immortal, the first part doesn't apply to Me."

"I've had enough of all of you," the Unbound Evil says. "The Devil is already in you, but I have no choice now!" The Unbound Evil dashes into Vizor. He's being possessed yet again.

"What is It doing?" D looks scared. "That looks gross!"

It really does look like a gross transmutation. Although, since I've seen this a lot of times now, I'm accustomed to it.

The Devil and Vizor are both, eventually, taken over. Vizor's eyes become a deep purple, and he exerts the energy the Devil absorbed. This is the Unbound Evil's last stand.

"HEHEHEHEHEHE!" The Unbound Evil is enjoying Itself. "Now, let the prophecy unfold!"

"No." I get It to stop laughing. "Let *my* prophecy unfold. This is MY fate, my destiny, controlled by my own will. There are no strings left for You to pull, Unbound Evil. You're going down! Guys?" Everyone nods. I turn toward my friends and family, and focus my energy on them. "Witness the force of all of our powers combined!" Everyone starts to glow - Griff, Rodger, D, Z, Mom, Dad, and Griff's parents. "Dark Spirit! Now's the time!"

"Right, V." The Dark Spirit is on the same page as I am. "Time to unleash the true power of chaos. Let's do it!" The Dark Spirit's power begins to mesh with the prophecies' power embedded inside of me. The powers of both lightness and darkness cross paths, and as a result, ultimate power is born! Enter PURE EXTREME V! My left eye starts to grow deep purple. Much like when I am Dark V, my hair color becomes a bright crimson, and I start to exert heat, light, AND dark energy. Everyone follows my example, exerting the same energy I do. This is a sign that we all have different ways of using this chaos power, and we're about to unleash all Heaven and Hell on the Unbound Evil. This is it guys. We either save the galaxy, or die trying.

The battle begins. The Unbound Evil starts by charging at me. It's trying to take me out first because It thinks that will make the others lose their energy. My family quickly counters.

"Take this, you fiend!" Z materializes a golf club out of thin air and throws it lightning quick, but the Unbound Evil emerges with barely a scratch.

"Come now," the evil bellows, "is that the best you can do?" It darts at Z, but the evil runs into something and falls hard. It holds Its head in pain.

"Ow. What was that?" It takes a better look and realizes that It ran into a tree. "I didn't see that! Who put that there?"

"Umm..." We all look toward the source of the faint voice that just emerged. It is D. Of course, he always loved the outdoors. He's holding out his hand, but he's so scared that it's shaking.

"Why you..." The evil holds Its hand out, and materializes Vizor's blade. "Come, all of you. Let's see what you're made of." I take my first shot and fly straight past It.

"Eh-em." It coughs to get my attention. It punches me from above, and I descend at a rapid pace.

"Rghh!" My dad flies toward me to catch me.

"I wouldn't do that if I were... Arghh!" The evil tries to warn my dad, but It ends up getting clobbered by the tree D made. "I will destroy that punk!"

"D! Run!" I yell.

"N-no," he stutters. He gets clobbered by the evil, and starts to cry as he flies backward.

"D!" Rodger runs to make him stop flying. "It's all right. Why don't you sit out?"

But D refuses. "No! I-I'm scared...but this is about V. I want to help. I have to step up, just like V did for the entire galaxy even if he was scared at one point. That didn't stop him. I love him too much, which is why I can't back out now! I've had nightmares about this Thing and have wanted to do this to It for a long time!" He points at the Unbound Evil. "This is Your end!"

Z hits him from behind with his magic driver. Oh! Now I get what D's trying to do. I also get why he is so scared. He is trying to be a diversion so the rest of us can annihilate the Unbound Evil, even if it means sacrificing his life. D, no more of that, because you're going to clobber It while *I* distract It. However, right now, it will be my pleasure to take a few cracks at It.

"Hey evil!" I say as It turns around. "Dodge this!" It easily avoids it.

"With pleasure, V. HAHAHA!"

"Now! D, Z!"

"Wait. Uh-oh." The evil spikes straight down from the impact of both the magic tree and the magic driver.

"Go for it, Griff!" His dad encourages him to take the opportunity to strike.

"With pleasure!"

"Enough!" The evil holds us all to a halt. "Your energies are all Mine!"

"That's impossible. Ugh!" My energy is actually dropping. So is everyone else's.

"I finally exploited your weakness!" The evil puts us down. "Your energy is vulnerable when it's unleashed! Farewell, all of – OW!"

Someone strikes the Unbound Evil with such tremendous force that It flies back fifty feet, maybe more.

"No, it can't be." As I start to become stable again, I see a shining figure in front of me.

"Melok?" Rodger realizes who it is. "How did you get here? More importantly, how are you in an extreme state?"

"I was ambushed by the Unbound Evil. It trapped me in Vizor's castle with a lot of Its little minions, but the power you guys radiated gave me this super form. The prophecies' strength brushed off on you, which in turn, brushed off on me. It's a real miracle. Thanks, you guys, for helping me have three new friends!" Griff, Rodger, and I nod. We look back at where the evil once was. It isn't there anymore. We hear loud grunting noises behind us, and we look at the horror that is now in plain sight. The Unbound Evil has revealed Its true godlike form. It is now a giant 100-foot beast that has the head and wings of a dragon, the body of a sea serpent, and the legs of a bear.

"BEHOLD, YOU WORTHLESS MAGGOTS, PURE EXTREME EVIL!"

CHAPTER 25

The Climactic End

So this is the Unbound Evil's true identity? Is this the first time It will be using all Its strength? Did It really think It could beat us any other way? The evil's strongest weak point is It's underestimation for everything It lays eyes on.

"I'm done pulling punches!" The evil's rage is palpable. "You've made a fool of Me long enough! Die, all of you!" The evil spreads Its arms and a shock wave of energy makes us all fly back several hundred feet.

"Ugh," I grunt. "So this is Its true power?"

–V, the Dark Spirit provokes me. Give Melok My power too. He should have the power of chaos.

–Yeah, You're right, I agree in a heartbeat.

"Melok!"

"Whoa...!" He regains his balance. The others rush back to fight the Unbound Evil. "Yes, V?"

"Let me share with you the Dark Spirit's power."

Melok's appearance changes a little bit. "Let's join the others!" Melok jubilantly fist pumps.

"All right then!" I give him a signal to follow me.

Let the final phase begin.

The battle continues. The Unbound Evil keeps sending out shock-wave after shock wave rapidly, so we all have to be on our toes. I try to locate a weak point on the Pure Extreme Evil, but find nothing. I have to improvise, so I charge directly at It to see what will happen.

"Take this!" The evil backhands me, and I fly into the arms of Griff's dad, which makes him fall back a little.

"Are you all right, V?" Griff's dad asks.

"Yeah, I'm good."

"Pathetic," the evil insults. "Your power is mine!" The evil sends out a massive shock wave, bigger than the ones before. It hits us, even though we try to avoid it. The power of the shock wave is divine, but our power is beyond that.

"GHAHAHAHAHAHAHA! Now you know the true power of divinity! The power to take another person's will by force, and there's NOTHING that can stop it!"

A great mist covers the field, and we've been drained of our energy…or so It thinks.

"You're right," I acknowledge, "there isn't. Well, not until now!" The dust settles and we are still in perfect condition.

"NOOOO! But I'm divine!"

"Perhaps, but we have one power that not even divinity can grasp. That's the power we have inside of us, and the power of the bonds we all share. Do You see now? Even in Your strongest state, You still can't separate us. Nothing can. I hope You've come to accept that because WE'RE NOT GOING ANYWHERE!"

"Ugh. I'll get you for this!"

"Not as long as I'm here!"

"And me," Griff says. "I've got my friends' backs!"

"Us too." My mom puts her arm around my dad's back.

"I'll always be here, forever." Rodger pounds his chest.

"You guys are like family," Melok adds on. "This is the end of the line for You, Pure Extreme Evil!"

Everyone charges, pins the beast down, and I place my hand on Its forehead. "What are you…? UGH!" I separate the Pure Extreme Evil into its original 8 parts: Vizor, the Devil, the Solar Prophecies, and the Unbound Evil. It's over. It's time to put It in Its place after all of these years. "GOODBYE, UNBOUND EVIL!"

I fly straight through It, and It starts to explode.

"WHAT?" the evil says in the midst of dying. "NOOO! How did this happen?"

"Simple," Rodger says. "You underestimated all of us. And You're going to pay for that."

"It's over for You!" Griff shouts in joy.

"Or so you all THINK!" the evil smirks.

All of our eyes widen.

"You're dying as we speak!" I point out the obvious.

"But this, V, is merely a PART of the My entire being! HAHAHA! This was a test for all of you...and you passed. Congratulations! But I'll be back, V. And when I return, you and your friends will face My true power!"

"We'll be waiting. And when You do... We'll be ready!"

"AAAAAARRRRRGGGGGGGHHHHHHH!" The evil burns to nothing and withers away into space. It's over. After all the dust settles, we have finally won.

"W-we did it..." Griff's eyes start to water. We look around and notice that the Devil has again disappeared. Behind Griff, we hear a grunting noise. It's Vizor, but he quickly loses consciousness.

My family looks terrified at the sight of Vizor. Then I remember that Vizor is technically the one who took my family, but I decide to shed some light on the situation.

"Guys, I know we saw Vizor that day at our house, but he had nothing to do with your kidnapping. He's innocent."

Griff's and my family are both dumbfounded when they hear these words.

"How do you know for sure, V?" Griff's mom asks.

"Because through this massive, wacky, and life-changing adventure, I've come to know what happened to Vizor and what type of person he is. In his own mind, he is probably around the age I was when you were all kidnapped."

"What?"

They're understandably confused.

"I don't bite." Z is still suspicious. "How does Vizor not remember the last six years of his life?"

"You just witnessed the Unbound Evil possessing Vizor, right?"

"Yeah."

"Well, all of the things Vizor did in the Unbound Evil's control, he doesn't remember any of it. He probably doesn't even know me yet. In fact, the Unbound Evil took away his home planet, and he may not even know it's gone!"

As difficult as it is to quickly grasp, Z finally understands how this can be possible. "I get it. Poor guy."

"Rodger, grab Vizor and let's get out of here."

I turn to everyone else. "Come on, guys! Next stop, home sweet home!"

CHAPTER 26

The Aftermath

We're finally back home after all of *that*. I'm glad. I learned so much from this adventure, but I still can't get something out of my head, the fact that the Unbound Evil said It would return, and with Its full strength.

It has been about a week since we got back, and Rodger has left Griff and me to our parents now and has resumed his position as a police officer. It's been bittersweet for Rodger because he had been our parent for almost half of our lives. It was hard for him to give up that role. The adventure brought us real close together, close enough so that Rodger will always be with us no matter what happens. Knowing that made it easier for Rodger to accept and move forward. We gave him a giant hug and he left to return to work.

Speaking of hometowns, San Jose and Zaptropolis are helping to rebuild San Francisco, and it honestly still looks like it has that old-style feel I remember and love. Also, even though Griff and I have separate families, we all still live together in our cozy little tree house. However, since there are so many people living there now, we are giving it a drastic expansion.

Melok went back to San Jose, and Electrox moved back to its city, Zaptropolis. The two cities are now getting along very well, and are essentially acting as one. King Tut has also gone back to Egypt and is resting in peace, finally.

Since the final battle with the Unbound Evil, Vizor is still unconscious. At this point, all of us are concerned about him, so my mom and

I take him to our family doctor.

"How's he going to be, doc?"

He shakes his head as if he has bad news. "It's impossible to tell, V. We can't do anything to see what's going on inside of him."

"Why is that?" my mom asks.

"Our imaging instruments produce blanks when we try to study Vizor's internal organs. At first, we thought our X-ray machines, ultrasound, MRI, and CT scans were all broken. As impossible as it sounds, I must conclude Vizor doesn't have the same internal structure as a normal human."

I stop him right there. "That's because he isn't."

The doctor's eyes immediately widen. "What?"

"You heard correctly. He is not human." After I say that, he immediately runs back into the room with Vizor. My heart starts to race because I think I know what he's up to. Melok did the exact same thing with King Tut.

"Mom! Come on! Vizor isn't safe here anymore!"

"Why not?"

"There's no time to explain right now!" I start running. "I don't want Vizor dissected!"

"Dissected? Hold on, I'm coming!"

We run into the room the doctor disappeared into, and I find exactly what I expect. There are all sorts of needles and medical gadgets around Vizor.

"What are you doing?" I pretend like I have no clue what he's trying to do.

"I'm bettering the knowledge of humankind. If we can understand this specimen, then we can learn about an entirely other race of intelligent beings that could be out there somewhere! Don't you understand what this means?"

"I definitely understand how exciting a possible breakthrough in science can be, being an astronomy and meteorology fanatic myself, but don't *you* understand? Harming a life form is never the way to go, ever."

"Are you defying the curiosity of mankind? Are you defying the way we do things?"

"Yes, because our curiosity should never be mutually exclusive from our morals. There is a better way." I answer boldly. "And I have the will to make it a reality, no matter what tries to stop me!"

"Oh, is that so?" The doctor snaps his fingers. Suddenly, two security guards burst through the door, pin my mother down, and trap me inside a gigantic test tube, much like the one back in Egypt.

"Ahh! Let me go!" My mother screams in terror.

"So what now?" I ask. "Are you just going to dissect me too?"

The doctor smirks. "Yes. Quite frankly, we're going to find the source of your power."

"Well I've got bad news for you, doc. The power that you seek can't be found inside my body. It's much deeper inside me than you and your little guard dogs here could ever imagine."

"If that's the case, then I'll dissect every living piece of you!"

"Is this what you want your life's legacy to be?"

"Anything for the advancement of human knowledge." The doctor pulls out his scalpel.

"Even if you do find the source of my power, your conscience will make you suffer and justice will hunt you down. You'll never get to see what it's capable of. Isn't that what you really want, to use my power to share with the world? That's the next step, isn't it? How's the world going to know how to use this power that only you know about if you're not around?"

The doctor stops, drops his knife, and actually listens to me.

"You're not a bad guy, doc, I can tell. Our family has known you for years. That's why we trusted you. All you've ever wanted to do is help humans. So do I! I'm here to tell you we can find a better way, together. That's how solutions to problems are found, right? People cooperating and finding a solution that everyone'll be happy about." The doctor looks down at his knife. "If you really want to help humans, then your first step is letting me out of this test tube. Please, doc! We can do it together. I trusted you with Vizor, now all you have to do is trust me. What do you say?"

"Enough with the morals lecture, professor," one of the guards says sarcastically.

The doctor cuts him off: "Let him go."

"Huh? But sir, he's dangerous!"

"We don't know that. He trusted me enough to give me a chance. Now it's my turn to give him one. He's right. Now let him go!"

"If you say so..."

The other guard opens the top lid of the tube, and I jump out.

"You," the doctor points to the other guard, "let V's mother go."

He also obeys. I run to my mom and give her a big hug. Then I look over to the doctor and ask, "What are you going to do with Vizor?"

He carefully pulls out all objects he had placed into Vizor's body and says with a gentle smile, "Turn him over to you."

"Why?"

"He's an alien, right? So we can't do anything to help him. All I know is that Vizor will wake up eventually because he's only unconscious. When that time comes, V, I trust that you'll do what you think you have to do to keep him safe. This information is between the two of us. I promise it won't leave this room, okay?"

"Thanks, doc!" I give him a thumbs up.

My mom and I wave goodbye to the doctor and leave the building with Vizor.

In our new car on the way back home, my mom asks, "So what're you going to do with that poor boy?"

"I'm going to treat him like he's my third brother." My eyes start to water. "I really do think Vizor is a good guy, and now I have a chance to see if it's true." I remember what the Unbound Evil had said to me about Vizor's role in this giant legacy of mine: *Vizor has a set of prophecies called the Shadow Prophecies...*

–Are you thinking about Vizor's world? the Dark Spirit asks.

–I'm thinking about how Vizor falls into this "legacy" that my ancestors left for me. What do You think? Do You know anything?

–No. I think we should just wait until he wakes up and tells us himself. Why think about what the answer could be when all we have to do is wait for

him to tell us what is so?

–You do have a point. All I want to do is explore the possibilities because I'm so curious.

–All right, well let's start with what we know. Vizor's your opposite, so that must mean there's an entire world out there that mirrors our world and the Earth. We also know that Vizor has his own set of prophecies, the Shadow Prophecies. So we can also safely assume that these prophecies have something to do with your legacy. The question is, how do they connect and why?

I can now see why the Dark Spirit wanted to wait for Vizor to regain consciousness. There are so many possibilities that it would be futile to go through them all. I guess it's best to just wait, otherwise this conversation might go on longer than the amount of time Vizor remains unconscious.

The Dark Spirit reads my mind. *–Oh, all right. Let's just rest now. We've been through enough lately, haven't we?*

With that, I nap in the car until we get home.

The second I hear the car turn off, I quickly open my eyes and turn to Vizor to see if he's woken up. I'm disappointed to see that he's still unconscious. I get out of the front seat and open the back door to carry him out of the car. My mom and I take the newly installed tree house elevator up to the front door and walk inside. As we do, I notice Z and D on the couch watching SpongeBob SquarePants. Oh, how that brings back memories.

"Hold on," I tell them. "Don't change the channel. I'll be right back." I hurry upstairs to a new room that has just been added to our tree house, one of the many new bedrooms. This tree house was just that main room with three cots on the side that acted as beds but now that there are a lot of people living here, we've made the place a lot larger, and added actual bedrooms. This first one is mine. I gently place Vizor down on the nice, warm bed so he can recover comfortably.

"Hang in there, Vizor."

I run downstairs to do something I haven't done in what seems like forever. I sit down on the couch with my two bros to watch some SpongeBob. I put my arms around them, and watch until my eyes are sore. I try to keep watching but my eyelids feel like they weigh a ton and I give in to slumber.

A few more days pass, and Vizor still doesn't wake up. One morning, I decide to sit down on my bed next to him and just hold his hand. At this point, I'm deeply concerned. After about an hour, I notice that Vizor begins to shiver.

–Dark Spirit, are You seeing this?

–Well considering there's nothing else to really pay attention to, yes. But I'm confused...how is he shivering if he's unconscious?

–Maybe it's what I had hoped.

–And what's that, V?

–He's remembering his past. But judging by how he's reacting to it, I don't think he likes it. Should we see what he's thinking?

–Sure. Maybe we'll even see his home planet.

I place my hand on Vizor's forehead. On impact, an incredible surge of energy rushes through me. "Whoa!" I shout in surprise. I scream so loud that my dad hears me and runs upstairs to see what's going on. Suddenly, a bright light starts to flash from my hand and envelops the room in a white mist. My dad and I close our eyes so we don't go blind. When we open our eyes, we aren't in my room anymore. I don't know how, but we're in Vizor's head, seeing the memories of his past from up above.

"What is this?" My dad looks around. "I hope this isn't outside!"

I can see why he says that. It literally looks like a meteor shower just came thundering through. Nearly everything I see is on fire. Even worse, to the far left of me, there's a giant wormhole. Where does it lead? I don't know for sure, but if I remember everything from that journey correctly, I don't think it takes you anywhere you want to go.

"No," I tell him. "My hand was on Vizor's forehead because I wanted to see what he was thinking. I have a feeling these are Vizor's most recent memories."

"No way! How did we get here?"

"I'm not sure, but let's watch. First, let's try and spot Vizor."

In a matter of seconds, my dad finds Vizor and his family. "Is that him?"

"Wow, way to go." I take a closer look at the person across from Vizor. "No way! That's his brother, X!"

Vizor looks terrified of his younger brother, as he is cringing and crying in fear. "X, w-what are you...doing?"

"What does it look like, big bro? I'm simply executing my plan!" Even from all the way up here in the sky, you can clearly tell that the Unbound Evil is controlling X.

"W-what are you...?"

"Stop crying! I'm simply trying to create a better world. Don't you see? Your world is corrupt, with too many fallacies. This world is heading down its own path of self-destruction, so I will give these peasants what they deserve. Who cares if it's immoral? Who'll punish Me? I AM DIVINE! Say goodbye, Vizor. HA!" The Unbound Evil then leaves X's body and dashes into Vizor's. Vizor then flies off into space. Instantly, we're booted out of the apocalyptic scene and are back in my room. As soon as I regain my balance, Vizor darts upward in fear and screams.

"What the...?" Vizor holds his head. "Where am I?"

"Good to see you're awake, Vizor," I smile.

"What?" He's stunned that I know his name. Since the Unbound Evil has been controlling him for half of his young life, I was expecting as much. "Who are you?"

Who am I? I actually really think about that for a while. I'm just starting to get to know myself better, and this first adventure is just the beginning. From my extremely rough childhood, to this moment right now, a lot has happened to me. I know the Unbound Evil's painted a negative picture in my head but with the help of all of the friends I've made throughout these challenging times, the thought of winning this war isn't just possible, it's within reach. Because if I've learned one thing in life, it's that your future ultimately depends on how you picture it and take control of it. This war's just getting started, and round one goes to...

"V. My name is V."